POUND

POWERTOOLS: THE ORIGINAL CREW
RETURNS, BOOK 4

JAYNE RYLON

HAPPY ENDINGS PUBLISHING

V2

eBook ISBN: 978-1-947093-21-8

Print ISBN: 978-1-947093-22-5

Cover Design by Jayne Rylon

Editing by Mackenzie Walton

Proofreading by Fedora Chen

Formatting by Jayne Rylon

ABOUT THE BOOK

The original Powertools crew is back in a brand new series!

When James was a kid, he aspired to be a superhero's sidekick. He's never enjoyed being the boss. Not on while working for the Powertools and not in his love life. Fortunately, his husband and wife are far better at assuming control than he is.

With each of his spouses stepping up to be the foreman of their own crews, James is left wondering what there is for a cute, hyper-organized, former construction worker to do in Middletown. Sure, he could play house husband for his spouses, and the rest of their sometimes lovers, while taking care of their ever-expanding family. But after decades of swinging a hammer for a paycheck, he's hungry for a higher purpose.

James has read enough comic books to know he should be careful what he wishes for. Because when someone threatens one of their own, he will do anything —including calling in some of their more qualified friends to help—in order to figure out who wishes they would turn around and go home before they've barely unpacked their moving boxes.

This is a standalone book set in the Powertools universe. All your favorite Hot Rods and Hot Rides characters will be making appearances as well. So come make new book boyfriends or hang out with old ones!

ADDITIONAL INFORMATION

Sign up for the Naughty News for contests, release updates, news, appearance information, sneak peek excerpts, reading-themed apparel deals, and more. www.jaynerylon.com/newsletter

Shop for autographed books, reading-themed apparel, goodies, and more www.jaynerylon.com/shop

A complete list of Jayne's books can be found at www.jaynerylon.com/books

1

────────

James sat behind the steering wheel of the sensible hybrid sedan he drove to and from work. He'd just pulled into his driveway after a never-ending day. He didn't have the energy to get out and inspect the damage he'd done to one of his spiffy retro hubcaps when he'd accidentally backed over a four by four on his construction site earlier that afternoon. It was probably just a scratch. At least that was what he'd told himself as he'd turned up the radio to obscure the metallic grinding noise the wheel made during his trip home. He'd have one of their mechanic friends at Hot Rods take a look at it the next time he was over at their garage.

He didn't want to give his husband or wife the satisfaction of saying *I told you so* since they'd gently pointed out that his teeny vehicle might not be that well-suited to his profession.

Okay, so its low clearance and stock tires were better suited to the paved parking lots of upscale organic markets than muddy, raw terrain dotted with construction debris. It reminded him of a termite trying to lift an entire log by itself—underpowered, out of its league, and too cute for all that mess and chaos. But then again, so was he.

James posing as a foreman of his own crew... It just wasn't a good fit.

No matter how hard he tried to force himself into a hard hat mold, it ended up more like attempting to stuff that square four by four he'd turned into a speed bump into a round hole that also just happened to be his ass. He winced, imagining being impaled by mega-splinters and the mortifying emergency room visit that would ensue if he tried something so unwise. Cringe.

Even a stunt like that would still be less painful than compelling himself to get up and go to a job he despised, day after day after day.

He'd barely survived today and it was only Monday. The thought of having to do it over again in another twelve hours made his stomach churn. Dread sapped energy from him, leaving him deflated. His forehead drooped onto his arms, which were draped over the steering wheel.

The twenty years or so he had left in him before retirement seemed like an eternity when he considered it might be like this all the damn time. He collected what scraps of motivation he had remaining and attempted to muster enough give-a-damn to propel himself into the house, but it was no use.

He probably had been sitting there for nearly a half an hour when his wife Devon rolled into the driveway of the house their friends Joe and Morgan had rented, which they were all sharing for a bit until they could figure out the long-term logistics of their move to Middletown.

Devon emerged from the monstrous black pickup she'd purchased. Somehow the sprays of mud over its sleek paint job seemed like artistic decorations instead of like battle wounds as they did on his car. They'd had to invest in three separate vehicles now that James, Devon, and their husband, Neil, needed to get to their individual construction sites each day. He'd much preferred it when they'd shared a ride for all the years they'd worked on the same crew together.

Despite his foul mood, James perked up at the sight of Devon. She was sexy as fuck for a pixie of a woman—who made him seem almost normal-sized since he was miniature compared to the rest of the hulking, studly men on the crew—and tougher than he'd ever attempt to be. Despite her diminutive frame, she hopped out of the truck without bothering to step on the shiny chrome running board, as he would have.

A cloud of dirt puffed from her construction boots, making James even mopier. She'd been doing sweaty things, bossing people around and being capable in charge and he hadn't been there to see it.

Neil pulled up a moment later, lurching to a stop faster than was wise on the other side of James's relatively micro-mobile. James might as well have been at the bottom of a canyon between their two behemoth pick-ups.

Out of place.

No longer a pea in their threesome pod. Instead he felt like a turtle trying to cross a highway. One that was about to get flattened. He wished he could pull his head inside his shell and hide, but that wouldn't save him from the reality barreling down on him.

This wasn't going to work. He simply couldn't do it. His guts knotted.

When Devon realized he wasn't getting out of the car, she rounded the hood and tapped on the window. "You okay?"

No. No, I'm not.

James nodded. He forced his ten-ton arms to unbuckle his seatbelt and somehow summoned the power to open the door before swinging his legs out.

Neil was there, laughing, to scoop James up and toss him over his shoulder like a sack of cement. "A hard day at work, huh?"

James grunted, though he didn't squirm out of Neil's hold. Not when all he wanted was to get closer to the other man. He hugged Neil's back as if there was any chance his husband would drop him.

"I have to admit, I never gave Mike enough credit," Devon chimed in as they approached the house, still blissfully unaware of James's rising panic and despair. "Being a foreman takes a lot of mental energy, to handle the management part of it all and then be a member of the crew in addition. It's a lot."

"Whew. It really is." Neil groaned. "We owe him a turn being in the center of attention next time the whole crew gets together."

James didn't argue with them. Not when he could hardly lift his head. Then again, this had never been his dream. Worse, he wasn't sure what had been. He'd sort of fallen into the crew, following along with his friends, and he was willing to admit now that being with likeminded partners had been the glue that had kept him there, not some burning desire to build shit or work with his hands.

Calluses had never truly been his style.

"It's rewarding too, though." Devon's excitement perked James up a little. No matter what, he was glad that she *was* happy in her new role, pumped about the added responsibilities. "Today we broke ground on the site for the spa at Kayla's resort. I can already see how it's going to blend into the woods with the stone façade and the gorgeous beams we chose. I love knowing that when we turn it over to her, it will be everything she's always wanted, and that I created it. I made it happen."

Neil nodded, the side of his face rubbing against James's hip. Now *that* helped him feel a little better. "I totally get what you're saying. Mike and I met with Giovanni today. We showed him several options for the tattoo shop and the entertainment complex. Mike is going to oversee the whole project, but with Giovanni's particular interest in the tattoo shop it looks like that's where my focus is going to be. The man knows exactly what he wants. That's going to make it a challenge to meet his expectations." Neil cleared his throat.

"You're going to do great," Devon reassured him. James had no doubt she was right. While Neil wasn't always the most serious guy outside of work, he was a perfectionist when it came to their jobs. He was going to be an awesome fit for a high-maintenance client like Giovanni.

James knew better than anyone that Neil excelled at making people happy. Himself included.

Devon let them inside while listening to Neil's description of the design modifications they'd made and how he thought he could bring them to life. Neither of James's spouses stopped on the first floor. After Devon kicked off her boots, then helped Neil remove his and James's while still clutching James, who was content to rest in his hold, they headed straight upstairs to the master bathroom, chatting the whole way.

Devon's shirt hit the floor. Her jeans followed as they approached the bright white tile of the spacious bathroom. He spied the claw-foot tub as Neil set him down, dragging James's body across his own, pausing only for a brief but potent kiss and a smile that made James sure that no matter what had happened at work, Neil was as glad as James to be home and spending time together.

The bands around his heart eased some, but not entirely. Especially when Devon turned to him, already mostly naked. A plum sports bra highlighted the smooth pale skin beside it.

"How'd it go today?" Her too-casual tone didn't quite conceal a hopeful note.

James wished he could give her the answer she so desperately wanted to hear. Especially since he was only tackling an insignificant project, a quick garage build-out for a client of the Hot Rods, basically filling in while the rest of the crew was busy with important shit.

It wasn't that the job was difficult or that he couldn't handle the management aspects—in fact, he was pretty kickass at that aspect. He simply didn't want to. His heart wasn't it in. That was standing right there in front of him, and no matter how badly he wished it could be different, he was going to have to disappoint them.

"I hated every fucking minute."

Devon's face fell. The glow of success and anticipation faded from her eyes, and he felt even more like shit. Not only was he miserable, he was making the people he loved wretched and anxious too. They were jumpy, on pins and needles, waiting for him to blow. So he figured he should get ahead of things and make a change before what they were all afraid of came to pass.

"Look, I gave this a try. It sucks. I'm not into it. I don't want to be a foreman. After this is finished, next week or whatever, I quit." James shrugged. "I mean, can you resign from your own business? Maybe I should fire myself or have one of you or Mike do it. Either way, I'm out. I'm officially hanging up my Powertools hardhat."

Neil cringed. "Are you sure? I know we're already separated, running our own projects, but this feels…"

"Worse? Final?" James scrubbed his hand over his face. "I know. But… Yes, I'm positive. I'm out." His shoulders slumped and his arms hung limply at his sides.

Devon plastered herself to his front while Neil surrounded him, embracing him from behind. They squeezed him tight, then began to strip him naked. But they didn't say anything.

"That's it? No one's going to argue?" James wasn't sure if that made him feel better or worse.

Neil shushed him with another kiss. "We can talk about it after."

"After what?" James asked, raising a brow at Devon.

"After we take a shower and wipe all this…whatever this is…out of your brain." Devon wiggled her finger in a circle around James's face.

He turned and caught his reflection in the mirror. Dark circles rimmed his usually bright eyes. His mouth turned down, and his skin was ashen as fuck. Stress etched his face, intensifying the damned fine lines that seemed to be appearing and multiplying on his face every time he looked at himself. Bad energy buzzed around him as Neil flicked the water on extra-hot.

This was one thing he wasn't about to argue with his spouses about.

Instead, he let them strip him and lead him into the spray to scrub the stink of his anxiety from his skin. If only they could do the same for his soul, they'd be set.

James closed his eyes and prayed they—and the rest of their friends, who were also sometimes lovers—weren't too upset with him and his decision to abandon the crew.

2

James sighed as he stepped into the shower. Warm blasts from each of the bazillion heads began to wash away his sweat along with his worries. Neil and Devon were right behind him, one on each side, keeping him steady between them.

"You can do whatever—be whoever—you want. You know that's not going to change a damn thing for us." Devon dodged the streams to glare at him as if daring him to say otherwise, to speak the fears he'd been harboring aloud so that she could smash them to smithereens.

"I know that. I do. And I'm grateful." James took her hand in his and raised it to his lips. He licked droplets from her knuckles before kissing them. He'd never imagined himself married to a woman or even in a romantic relationship with one, but she defied every stereotype he'd ever held and encouraged him to do the same. She'd made him accept that it was okay to be himself, no matter how different it made him from other guys he knew. When he bawled during movies, she held him. When she had a rough day, he baked her favorite cookies. They fit together seamlessly and made each other complete. The same went for her and Neil in their own ways. If it hadn't been for Devon, he wasn't sure he and Neil would have lasted. She was the glue that held them together, and they worshipped her for it.

Neil took James's free hand and held it tight for a few moments before reaching for the soap to lather up both him and Devon. Beneath the soothing swipes of his sudsy hands, James relaxed. His thoughts began to pour out of him.

"It's just that part of me feels like I should do this. I don't want to let down the crew. And it makes sense. I can do the job. That's not what's freaking me out. I'm plenty capable of handling this project."

"Of course you are." Neil gripped his shoulder "You're organized as fuck with your color-coordinated planner that maps out your day down to the minute—I'm pretty sure you even have a sticker for when you take a shit—you've got twenty years of experience on construction sites, and you can even communicate with pain in the ass suppliers without devolving into curses like Devon and I usually do."

James chuckled mostly because he did indeed have poop emoji stickers. Hey, at least they weren't scratch and sniff like some of his others. "Yeah. None of that is the problem. It's that I don't *want* to do it. Truth be told, what I loved most about being on the crew wasn't the construction aspect of our business but the hanging-out-with-you-guys part. The camaraderie. The stupid jokes we shared and the sexy coffee breaks too, of course. That stuff was what made me look forward to every single day. Now that the crew has expanded and we're all split up...eh."

Neil snorted at that as he *very* thoroughly washed

James's cock and balls before soaping up his own. "I'm going to miss those aspects of the job myself, especially the break time blowjobs, but I guess it'll make our off time that much more intense. Having to wait all day to fuck you two is going to mean I'm pretty damn horny by the time I can be alone with you."

James blinked slowly and tried not to get distracted by their husband's hardening shaft, although he nearly gave up trying to hash things out in favor of reaching for Neil. It would have been one hell of a distraction. "What I'm trying to say is that without you two and the rest of the crew, I'm bored out of my mind. This isn't rewarding. There's something missing. It feels hollow and pointless. I know that probably doesn't matter. I need to make a living so we can start building our own forever home together and live comfortably in it, like we have been until now, but...I can't do it. I can't. It's selfish and stupid, but I need something more than a job or it feels like I'm wasting part of my life."

"That's not dumb." Neil kissed James's neck, making him sigh and tip his head to give the man better access. Devon took advantage, going onto her tiptoes to seal her lips over his. He moaned softly and surrendered to her while Neil ran his hands over both of them, staring down adoringly. "I'm sure there's something you can apply your skills to that would also be rewarding for you."

When they drifted apart again, rinsing off, Devon suggested, "Why don't you come work for me. No, *with* me. Or with Neil. We can be a team. Nothing says all of the crew has to disband."

"How would I pick between you?" James shook his head. "Or would you have joint custody of me or some shit? No. Then I wouldn't be fully involved in what was going on. And it would undermine your authority with your workers, who would probably assume that because I have a dick, I'm the boss of us. That's the last thing I want, especially for you, Devon. You've earned this chance to lead your own crew. You're incredible at it and you don't need my help."

She opened her mouth as if to object but then shut it again, focusing on rubbing away the last of the bubbles from her short hair. Because he was right. That's exactly what would happen. Their whole relationship, people had deferred to him or Neil when they met the threesome, especially subcontractors or clients. And it was time she didn't have to deal with that bullshit anymore.

As much as James needed to be with them, she needed to stand on her own even more. And there was no way in hell he was going to snatch that opportunity away from her before she could prove to herself what he already knew: she was going to be an incredible foreman.

He had no fucking doubt her projects would be done on time, under budget, and exceed her clients' expectations, and she'd do it with fewer mistakes or accidents than any of the other Powertools foremen.

She stared up at him from beneath lashes dotted with crystals. If she was getting emotional, they both pretended it was the last of the shower water, which Neil turned off, instead. Devon said, "Well, no matter what you decide to do, know that we love you."

"And that we'll always be here to distract you when you're having a shit day." Neil snagged a towel from the heated bar, wrapped it around James, then slung his arm across James's shoulder. He drew him in tight. James's face mashed against Neil's chest as he breathed deep of sandalwood soap and man. Suddenly he didn't give a fuck about the future, when he could make himself feel so damn good in the here and now.

"*That* I will take you up on." James tilted his face toward Neil, smiling, his lips parted just a bit, which his husband could never resist.

Neil dipped his head and dusted his mouth over James's before nipping at his lower lip. Not especially lightly either. Hard enough to prove that he knew James could take it. Devon hummed and cozied up to James's back, rubbing herself against his towel to dry herself off in the most sensual way possible.

She snugged her arms around him, resting her cheek on his shoulder. "And hey, this feels final, but it doesn't have to be. Take some time, get used to our new life here in Middletown. Screw your head on straight. See what else there might be for you. If you don't find what you're looking for, you can always come back to the crew."

He didn't want to give her false hope. Better to rip the Band-Aid off. "It's over. I'm done. This isn't my path. I'm so glad it's yours. You were made for this. I'm not."

"That's bullshit." Neil was uncharacteristically serious. "You're plenty capable of being a foreman. You said it yourself. Don't ever doubt that."

James tried to hold his hands up, glad his husband thought so, but they were pinned to his side by plush terrycloth and the steel bands of Neil's arms, which he did not mind one smidge. "I swear, I'm not having some kind of crisis of competence like Joe was when he first came out here. Look, I know I'm not the most butch dude. I don't mean it in the sense that I don't want to be in charge of something. It's just that without the rest of the crew, I'm not sure construction is all that interesting to me anymore. I've been there, done that, and have the tool belt to prove it. You guys were what was holding me in place there. I've worked my ass off for years, and now I want something...*more*. Something with purpose. A job where I can make a difference. I've earned that, haven't I?"

Neil's face relaxed and he drew James to his broad chest, swiping the last of the droplets from his back with the towel before tending to himself. "Of course you have. And good."

"Whatever it is you want, we'll help you find it. Take some time for yourself, James. Get your priorities in order. It's fine," Devon reassured him, and cozied up behind him, so that he became the filling of a hot-girl-hot-guy sandwich, exactly what he liked to be best.

In that moment, the rest mattered a whole lot less. Because he had this.

James was the luckiest bastard in the entire world and he wasn't about to let his husband or his wife forget it.

He looked at Neil and slow blinked. Barely a heartbeat went by before the other man dipped his head and nipped James's lower lip before crushing their mouths together.

Even after all these years, it thrilled James that Neil didn't go easy on him. That he was sure James was strong enough to take whatever he dished out and then some. Especially now, when he was feeling oddly fragile, Neil proved that he wasn't. That as long as they were together, they'd survive this or any other hurdles life threw in their way.

Devon reached around and ran her hands between them, her palms caressing James's chest then abs while the backs of her fingers did the same to Neil. It wasn't long before Neil growled, then leaned over James's shoulder to kiss Devon every bit as thoroughly as he'd done to James. James loved being caught between them, a little smooshed as they embraced each other around him, surrounding him with their warmth and good vibes.

When Neil put his hands on James's shoulders and pressed, he knew exactly what his husband had in mind. James sank to his knees, still partially smothered with his face tucked against Neil's abs and Devon close behind him.

As Neil and Devon made out, James shoved the towel slung low around Neil's hips to the ground. He reached for Neil's cock, surrounding it with his still-damp fist. Neil groaned and his knees bent as if James had the power to make them weak. He cupped his hands around the backs of Neil's thighs, bracing him for what was coming next.

James practically purred as he nuzzled Neil's stiff cock and balls, rubbing his sparse stubble over them. The slight abrasion only seemed to make Neil harder, his cock twitching as a bead of precome emerged from the tip.

James hummed then licked the pearly fluid from the head, making Neil groan into Devon's mouth. She clearly approved, her lower half pressing against the back of James's head and forcing him closer to the man they both loved.

He'd never stop being awed, grateful, and so damn happy he'd found not only one love of his life, but two. Never had he expected he might find a man who understood him as well as Neil, and then a whole group of friends that accepted and embraced his unconventional leanings. But he wouldn't have believed—even if someone had showed him a crystal ball—that he'd fall for a woman in addition to a man. Or that one would be attracted to him given his lack of macho tendencies.

Devon dropped one hand to his head and stroked his hair as if she could read his thoughts. She was good at that. At sensing his emotions, when Neil sometimes wasn't as in tune with James's mind as he was with James's body.

Without Devon, they might have fallen apart.

She was the very sexy screw that held them together.

So when she massaged his scalp, using the pressure of her blunt nails to guide him, he went where she led. He opened his lips and drew Neil's cock between them, slowly, teasing the head as he permitted it to slide into the moist, wet interior of his mouth.

3

———

Neil's abs flexed in front of James's face and he grunted softly between kisses that were escalating from slow wet glides to more desperate smacks as he devoured Devon's muted moans. James went down on him, knowing that by pleasing Neil he was going to encourage his husband to pass along that passion to their wife, too.

A low curse interrupted their makeout session when he began to bob slowly and deliberately over Neil's cock, working his way lower on each pass until he held the entire length of it in his mouth. Most guys would be jealous if all the men in their sex lives were better endowed than them. Not James. He considered himself lucky because he got to enjoy the crew's cocks and what they did to him. Starting with Neil, who made more than a mouthful. He loved the feel of the heat and weight on his tongue.

Instinctively, James spread his legs wider, imagining what it would feel like when he got his husband hard enough and horny enough that he couldn't resist fucking

James another moment. It was then he glanced up, his lips stretched into an O around the base of Neil's erection. When his gaze collided with his husband's, he felt it straight to his soul.

Neil groaned, then said, "How am I supposed to resist you both? James sucking the hell out of me and you teasing me like that..."

James realized Devon had backed away, but only to do some torturing of her own. She sashayed around to his side so that she could put on a show for both him and Neil. It wasn't difficult for her to command their attention. He hardly blinked while sucking on Neil and staring at their wife as she cupped her small breasts then ran her thumbs over her nipples until they drew into tight peaks he wouldn't mind licking after he'd finished attending to Neil's balls.

She swung her narrow hips from side to side in time to a beat only she could hear but he felt. Her hands glided down her torso, over her flat stomach and abs that were more chiseled than his own. Though she sometimes got insecure over what she perceived as a lack of femininity, he adored her somewhat androgynous beauty. Hell, worshiping her during their coffee breaks was one of the things he missed most about working together on the crew.

James's cock stiffened as he thought about how many times they'd taken care of each other, getting extra down and dirty on a job site. Those days might be over, but he planned to make up for the loss with even steamier nights.

There had been plenty of times where they'd been too damn exhausted to move after getting home from a day, or week, of nonstop manual labor. Fortunately, Neil and Devon would now be overseeing their sites more often than swinging a hammer. Whatever he did next, he thought he'd rather it be more about his brain than his brawn, which—truth be told—had never been his forte, like it was with Dave or Mike or even Devon.

He raked his gaze down her fit form, lingering on her tight ass and cut thighs. She was perfect. Sleek and powerful, like a lioness. And though she sometimes complained that she wasn't softer or especially curvy, he loved her precisely as she was.

James dropped his hand to his dick, which was a dangerous maneuver. It would be easy for him to get too excited by the sight of Devon's gorgeous body or the taste of Neil's cock and come before things really heated up. While he might risk the more thorough enjoyment he'd take from fucking one of his spouses, he certainly wasn't about to take a chance that he might not live up to Devon or Neil's expectations.

Or worse, that he might finish too soon and fail to give them everything they needed to do the same. He admitted he sometimes had a hair-trigger. The upside was that he seemed to be able to recover far more frequently and quicker than some of the other Powertools guys. It was an especially handy trait when they were trying to keep going late into the night, which they sometimes did in order to fully satisfy their voracious wife.

And he wasn't about to complain about that.

Devon refocused his attention on her when she sighed. Her stare fixated on the place where he was connected with Neil.

"Jealous?" Neil asked her with a wry grin.

"Hell yes." She ran her hand over her mound, making James salivate. "He knows how to do things with that mouth I've only dreamed of before."

Neil groaned when James swirled his tongue around the tip of his husband's cock before swallowing him again. It filled him with pride that at least here, he could be confident about what the fuck he was doing. Neil withdrew the slightest bit. "Tell me about it. I could die happy with him sucking me off. You know I love you a hell of a lot if I'm willing to share right now."

Devon snorted. "Like you're not going to find somewhere else to put your dick."

Then it was James's turn to moan. He shuddered between Neil's legs and his knees spread as he unconsciously widened his stance.

"You like the sound of that?" Neil grabbed James's hair, tugging until he was forced to let go of his treat. Neil's cock slipped from his lips with a wet pop.

James nodded, relishing the slight pain of Neil's grip as he did. "Uh huh."

Devon smiled at them, then walked backward until her thighs hit the mattress. She scooted onto it and kept crawling in reverse until her head neared the pillows.

"Get comfy so you can enjoy what our man is about to do to you," Neil commanded.

Devon lay back on the bed, spread her legs, and crooked her finger. James flew to her faster than Nathan's puppy chased tennis balls. Neil instinctively used one hand on James's elbow to help him up then smacked his butt as he passed.

James tucked onto his knees, deliberately putting his stinging ass up in the air as he tipped forward and buried his face in Devon's pussy. He breathed deep, never getting tired of the sweet scent of her and how it contrasted with the earthy taste of Neil's cock. As much as James loved giving blowjobs, he found that teasing Devon, finding precisely the right way to lick at her clit, to be even more rewarding. To be honest, giving a BJ didn't take nearly as much finesse or skill, though James prided himself on his workmanship.

He'd made going down on his spouses an art form. Nothing got him hotter, faster, than bringing them to the edge. Knowing he could turn them on as much as they got to him did something to him. The number of times he'd made a mess of himself, grinding against the sheets while they came on his face or down his throat would probably have been embarrassing to some people.

Not him. He thought of it as a badge of honor.

He peeked up at Devon, gauging her mood and if she'd need him to start slowly or if she'd be impatient and greedy like she sometimes was when she had him and Neil to herself.

She speared her fingers into his hair, which was probably a bit longer than hers, and tugged.

Greedy it was.

James hummed against her dewy flesh. He opted not to indulge in light brushes of his tongue along her folds, advancing straight to surrounding her clit with his lips.

She gasped and arched her hips to seal his mouth more tightly around the sensitive bundle of nerves. So he sucked lightly on her, which spurred a moan from her.

"That's right. If you make her come, I'll let you have my cock. Would you like that?" Neil teased from where he watched, kneeling upright between James's knees. He tapped his hard-on against James's ass, bouncing it off the tight muscles of his cheeks before sliding inward to ride his crack.

James didn't bother taking his mouth from Devon long enough to respond verbally. Instead he rocked backward, attempting to increase the contact with Neil's cock even as he eased his hand between his chin and Devon's soaked pussy. He dipped a finger into her, marveling at how damn hot she was, then stroked her from the inside out, loving how she clenched around him, hugging him within her.

She didn't care that James craved getting fucked as much as any of the rest of the Powertools crew, or their wives, for that matter. Hell, she got off on it.

And that's when James realized that Neil was setting them up for a long ride, clearly not intending for her first orgasm to be her last but only a quick appetizer.

This was the warm up for the main event.

For the first time in weeks, James felt like he was right where he belonged. Like he was useful and competent and perfect for this position. He was made to give his husband and wife pleasure and to receive it back a million times over.

He added a swirl of his tongue to the hollowing of his cheeks, drawing on Devon's tightening clit.

She didn't wait for him to settle deeper into her either. She rose up, leveraging his mouth to get herself off. He loved that about her—that she wasn't afraid to take what she wanted or to use him and know that he would love every moment of it.

"You must be needing my cock." Neil chuckled from behind them, his thumbs spreading James's cheeks so that his dick could notch at the entrance to James's ass. It was pure, incredible torture, feeling his husband poised there, ready to penetrate, yet holding back because he knew it would make the sensations that much more potent when he finally sank inside.

Besides, they almost always gave Devon a head start since she could climax so many times more than they could ever dream of, and they often enjoyed testing her limits.

James didn't think it was going to be that kind of marathon afternoon, though. Not when each of them suffered the effects of working apart and living in a new and unfamiliar place. They rode a constant stream of uncertainty and worry that had them on edge.

They needed comfort. They needed each other and the special bond only they shared.

4

———

James added another finger and then a third to Devon's pussy, scissoring them to stretch her around his digits. She threw her head back and slapped the mattress so he did it again and again.

"Is he doing a good job?" Neil asked her, and James knew it was more for his own benefit than Devon's. He loved when they talked about him, praised him, and debated his most admirable traits. They pumped him up, raving about his abilities, when he didn't always feel certain of them himself.

Devon couldn't fake the way her body responded to his touches, his kisses, and his presence within her. She shuddered and ratcheted down on his hand some more. "Fuck, yes. He could make me come in ten damn seconds if he wanted to."

Neil hummed and petted James's flank. "Maybe you should do that, James. Your tight ass is looking pretty fucking good from here and I'm so damn hard from your mouth on me. I can't wait to fuck you."

James's cock jerked. He reached for it, but Neil slapped his hand away.

"Not until I say so." Neil took over, cupping his hand loosely around James's junk to prevent him from even rubbing himself on the mattress.

He had no self-control. Maybe that's why he liked it so much when Devon and Neil forced him to wait before granting him relief. It was ten times sweeter and more satisfying when they took him along with them. When they strung him out on unimaginable pleasure and let him stew in passion before granting every sensual wish he'd ever made.

"Please, Devon." James hadn't meant to stop sucking on her even long enough to beg, but the words spilled out. And she quaked in response.

"Need to or I won't last one second when he puts his cock in you." Devon stiffened beneath James, panting as she reached for her own looming orgasm. She did seem to get off on watching them fuck. Him and James especially, but all the men in the crew when they joined together too.

She truly was their soul mate.

James monitored her expressions and chased her most sensitive spots as she writhed beneath him. From behind, Neil chanted his encouragement to them both. And when Devon cried out, Neil didn't wait. He must have taken the opportunity to lube himself while they were playing, because his slicked cock was there, pressing into James, spreading him until his own pleasure-steeped shouts echoed Devon's. Neil called their names then sank deeper, fusing them in a chain of ecstasy.

Devon's pussy smothered James's fingers as Neil penetrated him inch by inch. When his balls were resting against James's stretched ass, he leaned forward to bite James's shoulder.

Devon cheered them on. "Fuck yes. Do it, Neil. Make me ready again so I can come with you two next time."

"You hear that?" Neil rasped in James's ear. "Our wife wants me to fuck you. And if you can hold out, maybe she'll let you fuck her so we can all fly together next. Would you like that?"

James whimpered. How would he ever last when Neil was riding him so well, his cock nudging James's prostate on every torturously slow pass?

"Would you?" Neil's question was sterner the second time, punctuated by another slap on his flank.

"Yes. Yes, please." James didn't think those spanks were having the effect Neil might have intended. Or then again, they probably were. They certainly didn't deter him and instead only riled him further.

Neil ramped up the pace of his lunges, fucking James until every remnant of his previous thoughts had been erased from his mind and the only thing he experienced was bliss. One particularly rough thrust knocked him forward and he collapsed on Devon, squishing her beneath him.

She didn't seem to mind, wrapping her arms around him and kissing the shell of his ear before murmuring, "That's right, James. Take his cock. Let him make you feel good."

"You do too, you know?" He didn't have a lot of sober brain cells given the intoxicating endorphins Neil was flooding him with, but he had enough sense to lift his face so that he could lay his lips on hers.

Devon was such a good kisser. She wasn't timid like he sometimes could be. She took charge and swooped in, doing what she knew would please them both. So he let her have control while he relied on Neil to hold him in place. His husband took what he needed and gave James the same.

Devon smiled against his mouth as she looked into his eyes from so close that he could read the love and acceptance in them. How he'd ever gotten lucky enough to find a single person that fell for him, never mind two, and a crew of lovers on top...he'd never know.

But he was grateful every day that he had.

"I love you," he whispered against Devon's parted mouth, and she swallowed his promise before reflecting it back in the gentle swipes of her lips on his, if not in words right away.

But when she came up for air, after Neil plunged balls-deep in James's ass, she echoed his sentiment. "I love you too, James. Always will."

His whole body clenched at that, including the parts of him hugging Neil.

Neil rocked his hips forward, pressing James tighter to Devon. She spread her legs and made room for his hips. His arms were pinned between them, but he wriggled until he could withdraw his fingers from inside her, where she'd started clenching on him periodically. He used them to stroke her breasts and her flat stomach until she began to rub against him.

His cock was trapped against her soft flesh, slippery following her release. Combined with the pressure of Neil in his ass, he hoped he didn't disappoint them and shoot all over her pretty pale skin before they were ready.

Neil growled and raked his teeth along the column of James's neck. "It looks like she's almost there."

"I am. It feels so good." Devon reached for him,

clasping his shoulders and tugging so that their chests mashed together. He liked that her breasts were smaller than the rest of the crew ladies so that they aligned almost inch for inch, their torsos connected everywhere. "I want to be joined with you. Both of you."

James hesitated only a fraction of an instant, long enough to glance over his shoulder at Neil, who beamed and nodded. "Go ahead. Do it. Fuck our wife."

As if that wasn't enough to make precome pool at the tip of his dick, Neil spanked James's ass, then grabbed his hips, lifting him and shuffling forward without disrupting their connection. Neil's cock stayed firmly embedded in James's ass as he physically positioned James in range to slide into Devon's waiting pussy. Neil reached around to stroke James's cock a few times, making James's head loll onto his husband's shoulder for a moment. Then he used his thumb to spread the slickness over the head of his cock.

Though James's erection was no match for some of the Powertools' tools, Dave's especially, Devon was so petite they were a perfect fit. He never had to worry about hurting her or going slow like some of the other guys did when they fooled around with her.

Neil set James down on his knees, then leaned forward, pressing James forward until he was in his most favorite place, sandwiched between his spouses. Devon hummed as their combined weight settled on her. She could handle them, no problem, and in fact had told them often how much she loved feeling them over her. Probably why Neil was making sure to give her the full force of them right then.

Neil leaned in, his chest blanketing James's back so that James felt completely surrounded by Neil and Devon, protected and adored. It would have been impossible to be anything but ecstatic in that moment. He wished it could last forever.

But none of them had that kind of stamina. Not when emotions were high and libidos were running wild.

Neil pumped James's cock several times, a little jerkily since he didn't have much room to maneuver. The uneven strokes only made them less predictable and had James jolting between Devon and Neil as if he'd accidentally touched his screwdriver to a live 220 line.

Then Neil used his firm grip on James's cock to aim him at Devon's core. And when James would have tilted forward, penetrating the tight, slippery ring of muscles at her entrance, Neil instead used his hold to tap James's cock head against her clit, making both of them moan.

He kept teasing all three of them, probably because he needed a minute to get himself under control, by rubbing the tip of James's cock up and down Devon's slit, dipping just the barest bit inside her before passing up heaven for another circuit along her slick folds.

"No more waiting," Devon commanded. She might be under them, but James would certainly never make the mistake of thinking she was helpless. The next time his dick aligned with her opening, she arched up, embedding him an inch or so within her.

The first contact was always so sweet it made him grit his teeth.

Neil banded his arms around them, then ground into James's ass, the motion fusing James and Devon tighter. Every millimeter deeper James's cock went in her, he felt better, because this was where he belonged. This was where he'd always been destined to be. The rest they could figure out together.

Neil chuckled sadistically, then put James out of his misery, fucking harder so that James wedged deeper into Devon. James went limp—other than his dick—allowing his spouses to fuck him, to use him however they needed most, and for Neil to fuck Devon through him.

As James's hard-on slid deeper into Devon's velvety pussy, he threw his head back. It rested in the crook of Neil's neck as he ground into James, forcing James to fuse tighter to Devon.

Devon ran her short nails down his arms, adding another layer to an already overwhelming deluge of sensations. And when she'd taken all of him and began to rock beneath him, Neil did the same from behind James. Neil's balls tapped against the back of James's sac and Devon's trimmed pubic hair rasped against his pelvis.

James's vision whited out as they overloaded him with rapture. He let go of every thought, every worry, and every fear, simply existing as Devon and Neil made love to him and each other through him.

He felt like a conduit, lighting up with love and lust, transporting it between the two people he cared most about in the world. Nothing could have felt better than that.

They must have felt the same. Because after a while, Neil roared. Devon clutched his hand where it was clamped on James's hip.

"I want us to fall at the same time. To be together in this." Neil's desperate cry made James realize it wasn't only him mourning the loss of their day-to-day connection. Somehow that made things more bearable. Knowing that Neil and Devon were chasing their own dreams, even though it cost each of them dearly, made him sure he was doing the right thing by finding his own way.

No matter what, in this, they'd be together. At the end of the day, they would come home to each other.

"More," Devon chanted until Neil lunged forward, forcing James's hard-on to drill into her. He writhed between his lovers, alternating between sinking into Devon and impaling himself on Neil's cock. Either way he went made his heart kick in his chest. Bliss exploded through his system.

When he had burrowed inside Devon as deep as he could get, Neil helped him out, pounding into James so that his pelvis tapped her clit repeatedly. The walls of her pussy hugged him so tight it took every bit of effort he could muster to shuttle in and out of her as Neil did the same to him.

It would have been impossible to last very long with such intense sensations bombarding him. Fortunately, it seemed his spouses were equally eager to fall off the cliff of desire they were rushing toward.

Before biting James's shoulder, Neil growled, "How close are you?"

"Very," Devon responded before James could so much as shudder in their arms. "Like...*very*."

And that was all it took.

James figured they wouldn't mind an excuse to let go when he toppled into ecstasy first. He poured his release into Devon and his ass wrung Neil's cock in time to the jets he pumped into their wife. Devon shouted and clamped around him in rhythmic pulses that milked every drop of come from his balls while his ass did the same to Neil.

Neil slammed into James then held deep, his hips

twitching forward, grinding against James's ass while he flooded him. It never ceased to amaze James that he could invoke that sort of reaction from these two people who were the strongest humans he knew. He could turn them into quivering, panting messes like himself.

In the best possible way.

James sagged, melting over Devon, who hugged him tight as Neil carefully retreated and cleaned them off before nestling beside them. He caressed James's back and kissed Devon gently if thoroughly before wrapping his arms around them both. Cuddled together, James realized his spouses had been—as usual—right.

He might not have everything in his life mapped out, but he sure as hell had this part perfect. With a foundation this rock solid, the rest wouldn't be so hard to build.

5

I t had taken James less than a week to finish off his
disastrous trial-foreman project. The build itself
had turned out fine. In fact, a friend of his client had
begged him—including offering a generous bonus—to
take on another similar job. James had declined, referring
the business to the main Powertools firm. With that, he'd
hung up his hardhat and tool belt for good. It felt weird,
but also kind of freeing.

While Devon and Neil were off doing their thing each
day, he focused on making their lives—and those of the
rest of the Powertools—outside of work effortless so they
could spend quality time together.

Tracking nine adults, four kids, a puppy, and all their
related appointments, client meetings, birthdays,
anniversaries, school activities, and who knew what else,
was practically a full-time job. Or would be for someone
less skilled at organization than he tended to be.

He cracked open his infamous planner, thumbing past
first his monthly overview, then his weekly calendar—
featuring color-coded task categories and, yes, cute but

functional stickers—past the daily pages broken out by hour for each of the crew members, and the tabs for his meal planning sections, until he arrived at his outstanding to do list.

James trailed his finger down the scratched off items he'd already accomplished this week. Finalize the sale of their old apartment. Check. Arrange movers for the non-critical crap they'd left in storage. Check. Set up new personal and business bank accounts in Middletown. Check. Manage the payroll and bill pay functions for Powertools as well as his, Devon, and Neil's obligations. Check. Research medical practices, general practitioners, and specialists—like an OB-GYN for Kate and a fear-free dentist for Mike—who accepted their insurance, now that he'd set up their policy and gotten everyone updated cards the week before. Check.

He also made notes to follow up with each person, get their final input on who they selected from his suggestions, and to start scheduling the appointments they needed. He would enter those in his trusty planner for the coming weeks. Then he'd automate a slate of text reminders to keep them from missing any of the visits he'd set up. No problemo.

Wrangling a group, even one as large and diverse as the crew, was a form of therapy for James. Taking their chaos, which could easily turn into anarchy, and tucking it into neat boxes satisfied his need for order.

Though he was efficient as fuck, it took even a planning master like James two solid weeks of commotion taming and a few days to recover before he was completely bored off his ass.

After passing all of the things he'd already accomplished, he came to the single, leftover task at the very bottom. *Have the Hot Rods look at the tiny, insignificant scratches on your car.*

Ugh. At least it would shut Neil up. He'd been nagging James about the ding since the moment he'd noticed the damage, acting like the whole wheel was about to pop off like the head of a dandelion in summer and lead to James's early demise.

Of course it was nice that Neil cared, but James unleashed an exasperated sigh as he pulled his car up in front of one of the open bays at Hot Rods. It felt like both a waste of time and one more reason he didn't need for people to look at him like he was less capable or less masculine than the rest of the crew. It had only taken an instant of inattention. That didn't mean he couldn't drive well or that he should have bought some big, stupid vehicle.

James was dragging himself from the car with a significant pout when one of the mechanics, who also happened to be good friends with the Powertools crew, came out to greet him.

"Hey! Glad you finally decided to take us up on our offer." Bryce clapped James on the back, nearly knocking him over with his mammoth paw.

"*Oof.* Neil and Devon made me. They said it's unsafe to be driving around like this." James rolled his eyes. "Are you sure you have time to look at it? I mean, it's probably nothing. Right?"

Bryce took a peek at the wheel, then cocked his head. "Uh, no. I'd call that a definite something. We might have to have Hot Rides fabricate a replacement for that mangled metal near the center of the rim where it attaches to the axel, but we can at least set you up with a temporary solution that will keep you from getting a flat or having your wheel fall off on the highway. Trust me, nasty car accidents are no joke." The big guy winced as he rubbed his thigh, and James instantly felt like an ass. Here he was worried about his damn pride when Bryce would probably give a hell of a lot to rewind and avoid his own near-fatal crash. "If you don't mind hanging out a bit and waiting, one of us will squeeze you in between appointments. It's going to be fun working on your ride. It almost seems like a toy compared to most of the cars we work on. It's so cute!"

Well, shit. James really didn't need his spouses to be any more worried about him than they already were at the moment. Or for something awful to happen so they could say *I told you so.* Or worse, if his recklessness caused them to take time and attention away from their work to look after him when he'd already left them a man down. Damn it.

"Not like I've got anything better to do." James shrugged. "Thank you."

He jammed his hands into his pants pockets, strolled inside, and let his eyes adjust. At least there was plenty of eye candy to keep him entertained at the Hot Rods garage. It brimmed with sexy cars and the sexier people working on them.

Alanso had an engine in pieces, each doodad laid out meticulously on a canvas drop cloth so he could service it. His husband, Eli, was assisting him in between filling out some kind of paperwork on a clipboard. Their wife, Sally, wore a hooded white suit covered in speckles of a rainbow of colors that obscured the curve of her growing baby bump as she washed out paint buckets. Bryce reclined on a low board with wheels, then scooted under a heavily modified antique truck on a lift, rejoining his buddy

Kaige, who was banging on something while cursing creatively.

James angled toward the last bay, where Carver was fussing with a piece of leather interior and his man, Roman, was installing what looked to be custom lights on a sick olive-green antique auto with exaggerated fins. James had never thought much about cars, but he had to admit, these would impress just about anyone.

He eyed the flat expanse at the lowered rear of the car as he waved to Carver. Hanging out with him and Roman was always comfortable and casual, which wasn't all that typical for James, who wasn't butch enough to fit in with most people's expectations for a construction worker...or even a guy in general. Carver was built similarly to him, if an inch or two taller, and was comfortable letting Roman take the lead in their relationship. Being slender and short didn't keep him from kicking ass in the garage or the occasional bar fight in their slightly shady past, though.

Roman and Carver were probably the most likely candidates for James, Neil, and Devon's new besties outside the crew now that they were settling here in Middletown permanently.

Sure, all the mechanics were polyamorous like the Powertools, but something about Carver made James feel less like an oddball in the midst of some seriously macho dudes and kickass women. Carver's unbreakable bond with Roman reminded James of how things had been between him and Neil before they'd met Devon, and gotten lucky enough to have relationship lightning strike for the second time in their lives.

After all, Roman and Carver had been in a relationship for almost as long as James and Neil had been, plus they enjoyed front row seats to the Hot Rods group sessions. Toss in Roman's "little" brother Quinn, who was bi and married to both a man and a woman… well…they understood each other and their complex relationships like few other people could. Spending more time with them and the rest of the open-minded people who worked at the Hot Rods classic car restoration and Hot Rides motorcycle garages was one of the definite perks of the recent shakeup in their lives.

James laid his hand on the shiny trunk and thought about hopping up on it to shoot the shit with Roman and Carver while they worked on the fancy vehicle, which definitely did not have any scratches or even a speck of dust on it, for that matter.

"You're not about to sit on there, are you?" Roman shot James one of those unmistakably Dom-type glances that made him squirm a bit. He barely stopped himself from responding, *"No, sir."*

"Guess not."

Roman scolded, "For Christ's sake, it's a one-of-a-kind, non-production 1951 Buick LeSabre concept, boy. This car spawned twenty years of record sales and launched an iconic aesthetic. Show some respect or I'll put you over my knee."

James put his hands out in an if-you-say-so gesture. It wasn't the worst thing he'd ever been threatened with. Especially not if Neil and Devon were there to watch.

He turned, planted his palms on the tool bench opposite it instead, and hopped, scooting his ass back. James kicked his legs, swinging them idly in front of him as he leaned onto his hands, arms locked straight, and observed the mechanics. There was still plenty of room to spare both on top of the workbench and between it and Roman and Carver's project. Sometimes it paid to be the smallest guy in the room. Roman never took his eyes off James, not looking the least offended about James's second-choice perch.

In fact, his approving nod and wicked grin seemed to imply he enjoyed it being decorated with man-flesh.

"Settle down there, Barracuda, or you'll make me jealous," Carver teased as he traipsed in between them, laughing. He turned to James with a twinkle in his eye. "Just kidding. I don't blame him for looking. You *are* hella cute."

Roman growled. He impressed James with his reaction time, grabbing Carver and drawing the shorter man to him for a kiss that had James wishing Devon or Neil were handy. Roman didn't hold back, completely possessing his partner. His mouth opened wide as he thrust his tongue into Carver's mouth and dipped him backward over an arm that was ropey with bunched-yet-trim muscles streaked with grease. Carver went liquid in his man's arms, letting him take whatever he wanted and enjoying every moment.

Whew. They were hot as hell.

"Oh, now you did it, James." Alanso followed the chiding with something in Spanish that his thick Cuban accent made sound even naughtier than it probably was from where he was elbows-deep in his rebuild.

"Work now, play later." Eli snorted with a shake of his head.

"Maybe it's time for a pre-smoke break, if you know what I mean," James joked. "I can go hang out with Tom and Ms. Brown for a while if you need to take care of some private business."

He was going to miss those spontaneous interludes with the crew. He couldn't count how many times they'd been in the middle of a job and someone had started something and next thing he knew...

James shook his head. He couldn't think of that now or he'd be walking funny until Neil and Devon got home from their sites that evening. Or maybe until the Powertools kids went to bed and the whole crew could spend some quality time together.

Thank God for the industrial lock Joe had gotten permission to install on the door to the finished basement they'd claimed as their play area.

"Do you see this mess?" Kaige popped his head out from beneath the vehicle he was working on with Bryce. "If we take that kind of break, we'll be here until we reopen Monday morning."

"Are you *sure* you have time to look at my car?" James winced. The last thing he wanted was to impose. "It's just a scratch..."

"It's not. Hush." Bryce tossed a rag in James's direction, which Bryce's wise old dog Buster McHightops tracked with his eyes while Bryce and Kaelyn's son's pup Professor Puddin'pop charged after and tried to destroy with adorable snuffles and exaggerated head thrashing. "Besides, you guys are doing so much to help us out right now, one baby car repair is nothing in comparison to the Hot Rods expansion project. I can't wait until we have more room to spread out."

Not that James was personally contributing on that front either.

"Speaking of, I'm going to walk over there in a bit and see how Joe's doing. How do you like what you're seeing of your new digs so far?" James wondered. One of his fellow Powertools, Joe, had been busting his ass for months to transform the site into a perfect, much bigger home for his cousin Eli and the rest of the Hot Rods gang than their current apartment above the garage. The project had already changed the crew's lives and Joe was determined to have equally as big an impact on Eli and the rest of the Hot Rods. "You know if it's not perfect, there's still time to change a lot of the interior finishes and tweak stuff."

"That's not what Joe said." Sally waved one of the paintbrushes she was cleaning. It seemed like she'd recently finished free-handing lettering on the dope black delivery truck from the twenties or thirties parked at the rear of the garage. "He told Eli that if he couldn't make up his fucking mind he was going to charge him double for every scope rework."

James snorted as he angled toward Eli. That sounded like Joe. Of course, he wasn't serious. "Yeah, right. Don't let him fool you. Your cousin is a giant softie."

"I don't need to know about his junk." Eli grimaced.

"Oh! Not that part of him. *That's* not soft at all." James practically purred, intentionally antagonizing the shop owner while mentally reviewing their schedules to figure out what time the crew would be home and if they should order pizza instead of wasting time cooking dinner and cleaning dishes before they could act on whatever steamy vibe the Hot Rods were steeping James in simply by existing.

The familiar, natural intimacy in the group made him miss his time with the crew all that much more. *Fuck.* Before he could think better of it, he let his feelings fly.

"Carver, what would you do if you didn't work together with Roman or the rest of your gang anymore?" James asked bluntly. Because neither of them was traditionally manly, he got the feeling that Carver had learned early on—like James had—the value of loyalty and people who would watch your back no matter the circumstances.

"Wow, that's a tough one. I mean, this is all I know how to do. And I like to eat. Plus someone's got to pay for the new place. So…if it came down to it, I guess I'd still do this but on my own. It wouldn't be nearly as awesome as it is now, though. These dumb fuckers make Hot Rods more than just a job. It's another home. The only decent one I really ever had. It's part of me." Carver flashed him a sad smile. "Sorry. That's the truth, though I don't think that's going to help you out."

"Yeah." James sighed. Maybe he really did need to suck it up and try crewing again. "I guess I should just quit bitching and help out on Devon's sites or Neil's. Whoever needs help for the day, right?"

"Or you could be a kept man." Roman tipped a wrench in Carver's direction. "I kind of like the idea of my man cooking dinner for me and lounging naked in bed, resting up for when I get off work."

"You barbarian." Carver snorted.

"I can't do that." James shook his head. "People already think of me as a wimp. I might not be some kind of over-testosteroned muscle man—"

"What's wrong with that?" Bryce flexed, making everyone crack up.

"Sorry. You know what I mean, right?" James tipped his head and Bryce nodded, smiling. He'd only been busting James's balls, which actually made him breathe easier. He wasn't treating him like he was fragile or any different from the rest of the guys.

This wasn't so different from what James had before, hanging out with these guys. Maybe he could fit in here somehow.

"I've got something to contribute, somewhere. I just don't know where or doing what yet." James rubbed the back of his neck as if he had a chance at eliminating the perpetual knot there by smooshing himself from the outside instead of fixing whatever the hell had broken on the inside. "I have to figure out what I want to do from here, and before it makes me crazy."

"Don't try to force it," Eli suggested. "You'll find the right thing. Give it some time. It's been, what, less than a month since you got here?"

In some ways it felt like forever. James didn't like the sensation of drifting when he'd had a purpose for so long. It reminded him of the time before he'd found the crew. His whole life had blossomed at the end of the long, frigid winter that had been his childhood and adolescence. A time he didn't even like to think about now.

"Yeah, I guess." James shifted then slid from the tool bench. He had to do something, *anything*, before his memories of his sister's tormented eyes—after nights spent with their relatives when their parents were absent *again*—and dread overwhelmed him. He reached for something comforting in its familiarity. "I'm sure you're right. So for the moment, I'm going to pass the time by reconditioning these. What kind of savages are you guys, letting these chisels get so rusty and dull?"

"You hear that, Carver?" Eli teased. "James is going to polish your tools. You lucky bastard."

James bent over the tool bench, well aware of what his ass looked like in his tight jeans. Over his shoulder he said, "Someone hand me some sandpaper."

With a whistle, Roman complied.

It was cathartic, getting lost in the rhythm of grinding the metal down, clearing away the oxidation, honing the edges, and making each tool bright, shiny, useful, and new. He wished he could do the same for himself as easily. If only there was some formula to follow, he could put in the elbow grease and get it done. Hell, he'd hammer it out all at once. Apparently his mind and heart weren't so straightforward.

James kept working at it until there wasn't anything left to buff away. The background banter of the Hot Rods helped him keep his mind from obsessing over darker thoughts while he worked. And when he was finished, he lined up each of Carver's chisels in size order in their leather holder, then oiled the outside of the case and tied it neatly closed, eyeing the rest of the messy and well-used implements that could use his attention next.

When he turned around, Carver and Roman were staring at him.

"What?" James glanced away, placing the case exactly parallel to the edge of the bench, damn near an inch border on both the side and bottom, his fingers itching to start in on organizing the ratchets tossed haphazardly in a pile nearby.

"I'm kind of embarrassed about the rest of this stuff now." Roman slung a rag over them.

"You guys use these things constantly. It's hard to take time out from actual paid jobs to do maintenance." James shrugged. "I like making them shiny and perfect again. Ready to use. I don't have much else going on. I'd be happy to run through the your workstations and take care of the rest of them in the garage too over the next couple of weeks in exchange for the work you're doing on my car."

"I have a better idea." Eli ambled over from where Alanso was grinning in their direction. "Why don't you come work with us? We're always needing help with stuff like this and repairing the machinery. Seems like that would be a breeze for you."

James wasn't the sort to have a big head, but Eli was right. He could do that in his sleep. It was fine to keep his hands from being idle when he was in flux, but not something he would look forward to doing every day. "I appreciate the offer, really. While the company would be excellent, I'm not sure refurbishing tools would have me jumping out of bed every morning."

Eli grunted. "Damn. Our loss, but I can understand that."

Roman teased, "I wouldn't be excited about leaving your bed any morning either. Hell, with Neil *and* Devon to snuggle up with and roll over on..."

"Hey." Carver snapped a rag at Roman. "What am I? Used motor oil?"

Roman chuckled. "If you've already forgotten how I feel about you, maybe we should take the lunch we skipped and lock ourselves in the breakroom for an hour."

"I just cleaned that table!" Kaige glared. "Make sure you disinfect it before I eat on it next. Or at least let me watch for my efforts."

"That would just be torturing yourself. Unless Nola will be home sooner than usual." James glanced at the clock. There were still a few hours left in the day, even for people who worked a straight forty-hour week, which none of his crewmates nor their entrepreneur friends at Hot Rods and Hot Rides did very often.

He figured business owners were the only people willing to put in a million hours a week to avoid working for someone else. And he didn't blame them. After being, sort of, his own boss for so long, he didn't think he'd do well taking orders from someone that wasn't Mike or Neil or Dave or Devon. He had an awful lot of criteria for someone without a specific plan.

James wiped his hands clean, then sighed. He didn't want to waste the peace that had come from doing something beneficial and familiar for a bit. "Well, I think I'm going to go check out Joe's progress and offer to help him if he needs me, unless there's anything else I can do for you all?"

"Nah." Eli jerked his chin toward the expansion site. "I'm sure my cousin will be happy to have your eyes and hands on the job for a few hours. Just remember, our garage doors are open if you change your mind."

James nodded and bumped fists with Carver and Roman as he passed them. "Thanks. All of you."

"What's going on in here? You assholes slacking off as usual?" Joe ambled into the garage before James could go out and find him. The rest of the Hot Rods gave as good as they got, but with the exception, maybe, of Eli, they didn't know Joe as well as James did.

James saw the concern hiding behind his jokes.

"What's wrong?" he wondered, and Eli paused, narrowing his eyes in Joe's direction before stiffening up.

"Oh, nothing major." Joe put his hand on James's shoulder, which only worried him more. "Looks like someone stole a bunch of shit off Devon's site. Vandalized some too. She wondered if you would come down to help her fill out a police report and an insurance claim."

"Son of a bitch!" James wormed his hand into the snug pocket of his pants and withdrew his phone. He hadn't heard her calls with the din of the mechanics' tools and constant shit-talking around him. Maybe being away from her was the wrong decision. Not because she couldn't handle herself, but because he wanted to assist if he could.

Eli stepped closer and dropped his voice, "Watch yourselves down there. I'm not sure everyone is quite as happy as we are that there's such serious competition coming to town."

"What's that mean?"

Eli hesitated, and James's heart stuttered. "The resort, the construction business, hell, even Giovanni's projects—the tattoo shop and the build out downtown—it's a lot of change for Middletown. Some people aren't good at evolving, you know?" Eli frowned.

James did know because lately he felt like he might be one of them, though he was doing his damnedest not to be. And he certainly would never sabotage someone else over it.

"Let's go." James angled toward his car, then groaned.

"Would you mind catching a ride with Joe?" Bryce asked. "It's going to be a bit before we can get to your poor little car and it's really not the safest to be driving it in that condition."

"Ohhh, really?" Joe put his arm around James and ruffled his hair. "What will you give me to keep me from sharing that tidbit with Devon and Neil?"

"A blowjob?" James asked hopefully. Not like he minded giving them, and his husband and wife would love watching.

Joe fist pumped, then said, "We're out of here. Come on."

Despite his calm exterior, he obviously didn't like even an ounce of trouble brewing around the crew any more than James did.

"Someone will run your car over when it's good to go," Eli promised him.

"Don't go out of your way. And if this means a late night, don't—"

"We'll take care of it. Don't worry." Alanso smiled. "If you feel the need to thank us, you can stop by again sometime to shoot the shit and we'll put you to work, like Eli said."

"Is that a job offer?" Joe's brows climbed higher.

"I mean, he *is* probably the most useful of you Powertools lot. No reason he wouldn't fit in as a Hot Rod, don't you think?" Roman added.

James drew in a long breath and let it out on a deep sigh. "That means a lot, it does. But like I said, I have no idea where I'm going at this point."

"Understand." Eli nodded. "No pressure. You know where to find us if anything changes."

"Thanks." James crossed to him and hugged his solid middle. He was tall and built as sturdily as his cousin.

It made him chuckle when Eli was a bit awkward, not knowing exactly how to handle his affection, and patted him on the back a few times. This move to Middletown was going to be good for them all, James knew it would be. As soon as he figured out what to do with himself.

At least, no matter what, he and his family were surrounded by plenty of friends.

"Say the word if you want some back up at the site. We can be there in five minutes," Kaige said with a subtle nod.

Joe drew James back from his cousin, then steered him toward his truck. "Come on. Let's go help Devon before you get yourself in trouble with your husband and wife. I feel like these mechanics are circling you like sharks eying a tasty tuna."

James couldn't help but tease, "Are you kidding? Devon and Neil would probably chum the waters for that."

A snort escaped Joe. "Yeah, you're probably right. Let's go help your wife so we can get home at a reasonable time and test out your theory."

Now that was a plan James could get behind. He held up his hand and Joe high-fived him before opening the truck door, boosting him inside then shutting the door and rounding the hood. Some guys might be offended by Joe's universal chivalry, but James wasn't one of them.

6

———

James finished writing a sappy note on Devon's napkin, then tucked it into her lunchbox just before she came into the kitchen. She kissed him on the cheek, but didn't have time for one of her famous hugs before grabbing the travel mug of coffee he'd also prepared exactly as she liked it.

It had pissed her off to have to deal with the damage to the two by fours she would need for framing out the section of Bare Natural that was supposed to go up next week. Irritated her, but it hadn't freaked her out as much as James wished it had. Or even a tiny bit as much as it had worried him. Something about the slash job had seemed awfully thorough. And even if it had been the bored hooligans she'd blamed, that didn't mean they couldn't very easily hurt someone by mistake on a construction site.

"Quit worrying. I've got this." Devon was already heading for the door.

She looked damn good in her ass-hugging jeans and worn work boots. A flannel shirt flapped open over a tucked in white T-shirt he was sure he'd be bleaching after she finished her day on the worksite. She might be the foreman, but that didn't mean she still didn't get her hands dirty sometimes. Devon wasn't the kind of leader to sit around and watch her crew bust their balls or the kind who would ask someone to do something she couldn't do herself, and probably ten times better or more efficiently, for that matter.

For a moment, James debated again whether he should take her up on the offer to join her crew. At least then he'd get to spend his days with her, if not Neil too. Plus keep an eye out for anything not quite kosher. But deep down he knew those times were gone.

Worse, as much as he had enjoyed playing house husband to his spouses these past few weeks, it was going to take more than keeping their living space spotless, cooking for them, and managing every aspect of their busy, extended household to prevent him from losing his mind out of sheer boredom.

"Have a good day at work." He jogged to catch up to his wife, then handed Devon her lunch.

"I will. We're going to grade for the spa foundation today, so we should make some real progress. Then I'll really be able to show Kayla how the building will impact the rest of the resort layout with the parking lot and everything. Hopefully she doesn't think it impedes the view of the lake from the entrance too much or have too many adjustments after that." Devon rolled her eyes, though James knew she'd work on the project until it was as perfect as she could make it for her best friend.

"Where's Neil?" James asked, glancing at the clock.

"Going to be late to his own damn job site. Unlike me. Gotta go. Love you." Devon grimaced and shook her head once before kissing James one last time, squeezing his ass, then trotting out the door.

"I heard that!" Neil clunked down the stairs, grabbed the egg sandwich and sickly sweet soda he preferred to coffee, then kissed James. It was no peck on the cheek, either. He took extra time for tongue and grinding that would lead to him being really, really late if they weren't careful. When he pulled away, he scanned James from head to toe, grinning at the sight of his T-shirt. "You *are* my Boy Wonder, you know?"

James glanced down at the retro Robin graphic complete with a BLAM and POW plastered across his chest and giggled. It was no secret he'd always envied the character, who was by far the more interesting of the dynamic duo—a true and loyal hero willing to help out in all of Batman's schemes, no matter how hairy the situation. Plus he wouldn't mind getting tied up with his partner, who would be sporting a package-revealing costume, at some point in each of their adventures.

He wondered if there were any job postings in Middletown for an uber capable, supportive if bite-sized sidekick willing to work in the background for a superstar hero who operated outside of traditional law enforcement channels saving innocent people, kicking bad guys' asses, and looking hot while doing it.

Probably not, huh?

Too bad or he could have lived out every single one of his childhood dreams.

Neil rattled the breakfast James had prepared, snapping him out of his wandering thoughts. "I'll thank you properly for this tonight. Promise."

"I'm going to hold you to that." James grinned. He watched Neil amble out the door and climb into his truck.

James sighed and rested the small of his back against the kitchen island. He had the entire place to himself. For half a second, he thought about going upstairs and taking care of the insta-boner his hot husband and wife had unwittingly left him with, but figured waiting for sex in the shower with them later was way better than taking matters into his own hands, even if he could do it immediately.

So he grabbed his own coffee and a muffin then sat at the kitchen table and opened his laptop. He browsed the news, but shut that down quickly after seeing a lot of terrible shit he couldn't do anything about. He flipped through his emails, unsubscribing to junk mail and tidying his inbox before landing on a message from an internet site he'd joined to find out more about the local scene.

It had turned out to be more of a nosy neighbor bitching session than the cooperative hangout he'd envisioned, but it could be good for a laugh or two if nothing else.

James rolled his eyes when he saw a message with the entirely capitalized subject line SUSPICIOUS VEHICLE, which after reading appeared to him to be a prime example of someone looking for an address in a suburb they'd never visited before. They'd probably been trying to deliver flowers or something equally harmless.

The next post was of a woman asking if anyone had heard gunshots. Someone had posted a link to an online edition of the police scanner before a resident from a few houses down had apologized for their car backfiring. With a groan and a shake of his head, James clicked the scanner link. Unsurprisingly, for a low-key place like Middletown, there wasn't much going on.

Some chatter about roadside assistance and a speed violation. That was it.

Nothing exciting, and no calls for someone to save the city. So he gave up, licking his fingers before putting his dishes in the washer and cleaning the rest of the kitchen.

He verified in his planner that his entire day was one big blank blob with an inspirational sticker that said, "The best is yet to come."

James refused to sit around all day waiting for the crew to come back and getting blobbier by the second. Worse yet, he was afraid he might turn into one of the people peeking out their front curtains, bored enough to see things that weren't there, so he put on his sneakers. Without any real plan on where to go, he started trekking through the woods that housed not only Hot Rods car restoration garage and the future site of Kayla's resort—including what would be their new homes nearby—but, a bit down the road, Hot Rides, too.

If James couldn't have his husband and wife around as often as he liked, he might as well spend time with people who had what he used to: a business where they worked hard and played even harder. Hot Rods obviously fit that bill, but he'd already bugged them enough for one week. He zipped his jacket up higher and jammed his hands in his pockets. It was getting colder every day. Golden leaves rained down around him and crunched under his sneakers as he walked.

As he rounded a corner in the road, the sound of an approaching engine started out as a purr then grew to a roar that rattled the entire forest. He glanced over his shoulder in time to spot a gleaming black machine gunning toward him.

Jeebus. James jumped back as the motorcycle skidded

to a stop on the shoulder a few feet from him, pebbles attacking his shins through his calf-hugging jeans. At least he could wear more fashionable clothes now that he didn't have to worry about being able to maneuver around a construction site.

The rider flipped up the visor on his helmet and grinned. It was Quinn, the Hot Rides manager and head mechanic. Roman's not-so-little bro. "Want a ride?"

"Not if you drive like that." James shook his head. "I don't have a death wish."

"Come on, get on." Quinn teased, "Unless you're afraid that holding on to a real man will put you off that husband of yours."

James rolled his eyes. "Don't let Neil hear you talking shit like that or he'll teach you a thing or two, whippersnapper."

Quinn barked out a laugh. James couldn't deny that where he sat, with his gleaming black riding boots planted in the gravel, he had grown into a strong and confident man, completely unlike the wary, abused boy they'd met so many years ago when Roman had first rescued him from a hellish upbringing.

What the fuck? Keeping from getting stagnant had been the whole point of getting out of the house, right?

Quinn took one gloved hand from the straight handlebars and curled his fingers into his palms, beckoning, so James did as he was told. He climbed up behind Quinn, straddled man and machine, then clutched him koala-style. Maybe he should talk Devon into getting a motorcycle for Christmas.

"Should I go directly there or opt for the scenic route?" Quinn asked over his shoulder.

James grinned. "Take the long way 'round."

"That's what I'm talking about." Quinn nodded once, put his visor down, then revved the engine before taking off more gracefully than he'd slid to a halt. It was still plenty fast for James, who felt like he was shooting through the forest strapped to a rocket.

You know, a decidedly sexy, muscular rocket.

He was not about to complain.

7

———————

James had only slightly relaxed his death-grip on Quinn's eight-pack and let out a few whoops before they swung into the Hot Rides driveway. They rolled to a gradual stop, proving Quinn had finesse even if he didn't always choose to use it. When James hopped down, he vibrated with adrenaline, feeling really alive for the first time—outside of the bedroom—for a while.

Quinn took his helmet off, climbed from the bike, and shook his head, grinning. "I should have warned you it's addictive."

"Are we going to be working on a bike for James soon?" a deep voice rumbled from the direction of the garage. Trevon, Quinn's husband, emerged, wiping his oil-slicked hands on a rag that he stuffed in the back pocket of his dark wash, low-riding jeans. Quinn had done pretty damn well for himself, falling in love with two very capable, kind, and super-hot people.

Seeing the two men embrace casually, Quinn's fair arm decorated with colorful ink a stark contrast against the rich mahogany of Trevon's skin, made James's heart flutter for them both and their wife, Devra, who had escaped her war-torn homeland in the Middle East before discovering her perfect loves. They were different yet alike, and finding each other had saved all three of them.

Trevon turned back toward James and took a long look, as if mentally measuring him. "I bet I could find just the thing for you. Nothing too bulky, but something quick and agile."

"Oh, I don't…" James waved his hands in front of him, but then stopped. Why not? He could drive a motorcycle if he wanted. Maybe Devon and Neil would want to ride behind him. Plus he could justify buying himself a whole new leather wardrobe. This was exactly what he'd been telling Devon he needed to do. Expand his horizons, find things he might enjoy that he'd never considered. Grow into the person he'd always dreamed of being—bolder and in control.

"Well, why don't you keep your eyes open and show me what you come up with?" James nodded.

"What's that?" Devra followed a few steps behind Trevon, her hand slipping easily into his before Quinn entwined his fingers with her other one. "Don't tell me you're going to corrupt the Powertools now too."

Quinn's smile didn't fade any as he took in his husband and wife, who were incredibly gorgeous together. Devra's long, thick onyx hair blew gently in the breeze, curtaining them where they stood on either side and slightly behind her. James knew exactly how the younger man felt as he took turns kissing each of his spouses quite thoroughly. "I've been told I'm good at it."

Devra blushed a bit and Trevon snorted. Everyone knew Quinn had bridged the gap between the previously married-on-paper-only couple, opening their eyes to an unconventional love that they were eager to fully participate in. Quinn had transformed their entire universe and in turn they had fixed parts of him that even Roman hadn't been able to repair.

"So what were you heading this way for, anyway?" Quinn asked as he swung around again, wrapping one arm around Devra's tiny waist and Trevon grasping his hand.

"Uh, I'm not really sure." James shifted. "I'm bored and looking for something to do, I guess."

At that, two bruisers, who seemed better suited to a motorcycle gang than a repair shop, edged in their direction. Ransom and Levi hung out there a lot. After all, they were living with Sevan—one of Quinn's star mechanics—since their cover had been blown when they busted her step-father's illegal empire.

The Hot Rides' resident welder, Wren, was married to two guys of her own. One was a country rock star and the other happened to be an ex-federal agent turned all-around badass heading up a private security firm. Jordan was Ransom and Levi's boss.

James was pretty sure the sort of jobs they took on had nothing in common with petty vandalism, but no one asked many questions about the specifics of their business, so he didn't either.

"Did I hear there was some bullshit down at Devon's site yesterday?" Ransom wondered.

"Yeah, she's not concerned except for the delay it might cause the next phase of the project."

"And you?" Levi asked.

James shrugged, glad to be able to let the tendrils of doubt that had been worming around in his gut escape.

"It's another round of insurance claims I need to file and track and, really, what kids hang out down there anyway? It's pretty isolated. Tom owns the land around it for quite a ways, doesn't he?"

"Yeah, he does. Good point." Quinn frowned.

"Jordan texted me about it this morning." Ransom frowned. "He recommends installing some security cameras on your sites. He already ordered the equipment and said he'd have our guys do it tomorrow except we're... uh...busy with something kind of big."

"Uh, okay. Sounds good." He wasn't about to turn away any protection for Devon, the rest of the crew, or their new venture in Middletown. "It's probably nothing, but I like the idea of adding surveillance. If it's just a matter of running wires and standard electrical stuff, I'm sure I could put them in."

Levi nodded, whipped out his phone, and started texting.

"Never hurts to have extra eyes on things. Now that you're in Middletown, you've got a lot of friends around. We take care of our own." Quinn stood taller.

"I'm proud of the man you've become, you know that?" James patted Quinn on the chest, remembering the guy when he'd been an awkward and sometimes confused teen.

"Thanks, Uncle James," Quinn said with a jaunty grin that set them all laughing and dispersed the heaviness that had been intruding on their visit.

"Jordan says he'll hand the camera kits off to us tonight during our meeting." Levi told James. "I'll bring them over to your place and leave them on the porch before morning along with some instructions and the information you'll need to link them to our network so someone can monitor the feeds. He said you should call him if you have questions."

"Great, thank you." James appreciated the extra safeguards and someone watching the crew's backs, especially if he wasn't going to be around them to do it himself.

"So...were you serious about being bored?" Trevon asked James. "Because I, uh, could maybe use someone who knows how to build shit and make it strong."

"Did you put your big-ass toolbox on that rickety shelf again this morning?" Quinn cracked up. "I told you it was going to bust."

"Well, you don't always have to be right." Trevon knocked his shoulder into Quinn's, though he seemed sheepish about having caused damage, unintentional or not. "Besides, you never complain about the size of my tools any other time."

"True enough." Quinn squeezed Trevon's hand as Devra shot them both lovey-dovey eyes.

James knew what it was like to feel like you might not belong, even if everyone around you insisted you did. "Help me rummage up some tools from Gavyn's shed and I'll tell you all about the fuck-ups your hubby has made since I've known him. Remember that time you accidentally cheated on your girlfriend with her own brother after the prom?"

Ransom and Levi groaned and laughed, ragging on Quinn for being a dirtbag in his misguided youth.

No way was Trevon going to be the odd man out on James's watch. He strutted over to Trevon, snatched his hand from Quinn, then led him to the red-and-black outbuilding James and Neil had erected on a previous weekend trip to Middletown.

Behind them, Devra turned to Quinn and playfully smacked his gut before hissing, "You didn't really do that did you? You asshole."

Quinn winced. "Still not a proud moment all these years later. Ugh. I promise I learned to be a better man for you two." He drew Devra to him and showed her with a gentle, sensitive kiss that he'd matured plenty since then.

Trevon shook his head as James dragged him inside and pointed to the stuff he needed before they got off track and forgot about their project entirely. When they were both loaded down with saws, hammers, drills, and fasteners, plus a decent number of scrap boards, James figured he could whip them into something that was both useful and presentable for the shop before the afternoon was over.

"You need a hand?" Trevon asked as he set the load down near the wimpy AF shelf that had been obliterated by whatever mechanical whosie-whats-it Trevon had plunked onto it.

"Nope." James shooed him away. "You go over there, fix things, and look sexy doing it."

"Don't be looking at my husband's fine ass when he's bending over," Devra teased James as she returned from restocking the homemade snacks she spoiled them with in the breakroom. "That's *my* job!"

From around the garage, Wren, Ollie, Walker, Dane, and Sevan—the rest of the Hot Rides gang—snickered.

"Noted." James shook his head, thinking how much like the crew they were—open, loving, and accepting, along with a hint of naughty spice that would probably sneak up and burn you from the inside out until you were dying for a glass of cool water, or a solid orgasm, to quench your thirst.

So why didn't he feel at home here like he did when working alongside Mike, Joe, Dave, Neil, and Devon? Because the Hot Rides were a gang, but they weren't *his* crew and never would be.

James clenched his borrowed hammer and drove in a nail with two even swings. The familiar zing that traveled up his arm settled his anxiety, so he did it again, then again. He lined up a board, measuring it by eye, then sliced his pencil over it before trimming it to size.

What had been a single insufficient shelf quickly became an entire organization system with hooks for hanging tools beneath it and a cabinet that stabilized the entire unit. He anchored it to the cinderblock wall, which allowed for it to easily hold fifty times the load it had before.

While he worked, he didn't have to think about anything but creating. Tidying and improving. Building instead of tearing stuff down. That at least was something familiar and soothing. But it wasn't enough, because doing this well wasn't the same as wanting to do it all the time.

He made it a game where he played against himself, trying to do things the most efficiently, to the best of his ability, which kept driving him forward. In addition to construction, he was great at coming up with systems for things. Hell, even his underwear drawer was color-coded. So this really ticked all his boxes. He measured each of Trevon's tools, then custom fit the dividers in a drawer to cradle each of them perfectly.

Pretty soon, he couldn't think of anything else to add to make the project better.

He stepped back and eyed his handiwork.

"Damn, James." Trevon clapped an oversized hand on

his shoulder, knocking him forward a bit in the process. "That's incredible. I never could have imagined something like that but it kicks ass. There's a place for everything and I can see what I have to work with at a glance. This is going to save me so much time and aggravation. Seriously. Thank you."

Quinn stood shoulder to shoulder with them, admiring the new addition. "I admit it, I'm kind of jealous. You know, we always have shit like this come up."

He waved at the storage racks. "Something falls apart, or someone crashes a bike into an equipment stand —*ahem, Dane*—or we want to add a feature to the shop, but we never have downtime to do it right. We've been slammed with new customers and never have a chance to expand properly. If you're not wanting the hassle of a crew of your own, we'd be glad, and really fucking lucky, to have you here at Hot Rides working on...whatever."

"Are you offering me a job?" James wasn't sure if he should be flattered or horrified. He didn't need Quinn's pity or a spot as a lackey on someone else's team. What he wanted...well, shit, wasn't that the problem? He wanted what he'd had and that was gone.

Trying to replace it with something similar but not... well, it didn't hold the same appeal. Not without some higher purpose. It might make him a fool to keep searching for something he couldn't put his finger on. Shouldn't he be grateful for what he'd had and do his best to contribute what he could going forward?

He must have hesitated too long.

"I mean...only if you want one." Quinn held his hands up, palms out.

"Thanks, Quinn. I do appreciate the thought, but..."

"Ah, he's letting you down easy." Sevan patted her boss on the shoulder. "That was a good try, though, Quinn."

"Yeah, we probably couldn't afford him anyway." Trevon smiled kindly at James. "You're *really* great at this."

"Thanks." He scanned his work. It had been a quick build and, yeah, it didn't totally suck. But what did you do when you didn't want to do the thing you were best at anymore?

He looked up at the clock and saw they'd been at it longer than he'd realized. Neil and Devon would be home soon enough. And no matter what else he was unclear about in his life, he knew that he wanted to spend as much time with them as he could. "I think I'd better head back to our place if I'm going to get there before the rest of the crew comes home."

"Want a ride?" Quinn offered.

James figured he'd had enough new experiences, and rehashed ones, for that day. None of them seemed quite right, and it only made him feel like a would-be Cinderella who couldn't make the construction boot fit.

"Nah. The fresh air and some exercise will do me good." James went over and hugged Quinn and Trevon, Sevan too for the hell of it, making sure they knew there were no hard feelings and his weird mood was all his own doing, not theirs. He thought of Quinn like family. His lovers and the rest of his gang were an extension of him. James would make it up to them next time he saw them, when he'd hopefully have his head on straight again.

"Are you getting ready to leave? Hang on just a minute." Devra held up a finger as she trotted toward their tiny home down the picturesque path from the garage. It was a setup the Powertools were drawing inspiration from for their own complex of not-so-tiny houses on the lake beside Kayla's new resort and spa.

Devra returned in a minute with a backpack and pressed it into James's hands. He smelled the treats inside before he peeked in. "Is it that obvious that I need some carbs?"

She nodded, then flung her arms around him before Quinn and Trevon piled on, surrounding him in their warmth.

"I'm going to be fine. Everything's fine," James reassured exactly no one as he untangled himself from their comfort.

"We'll make sure it is. Let Jordan know if you need assistance with the camera install tomorrow and I'm sure he'll find someone to help," Ransom reminded him.

"I'll figure it out, no worries." James waved and turned toward the house the Powertools were staying in, which didn't yet feel like home, even more annoyed with himself and unsure of where to go next.

8

———————

When James made it back, Joe had beaten him home and was taking the opportunity to mow the lawn before the rest of the crew arrived. The days grew shorter and the trees on the perimeter of the yard had already lost all their leaves as time zoomed toward Thanksgiving, but it had been unseasonably summery lately.

Yay for global warming?

The hum of the mower and the fresh scent of shorn grass helped buoy James's spirits. It was nearly as good as a whiff of sawdust, which had become bittersweet for him lately. The comfort food he was preparing for the Powertools' dinner would help too.

He set the meatloaf that had just finished baking on the counter right as the front door opened. Kate came inside followed by a train of people made up of her kids, Morgan and Joe's kids, and then Morgan. Nathan's puppy, who was growing faster than a pile of sawdust underneath a drum sander, bounded in too.

"Hey, perfect timing." He tried not to roll his eyes at

himself, realizing how much like the *house husband* option Roman had teased him with the day before he was resembling at the moment. No, this wouldn't do either. It was fun to spoil the crew for a little while, sure. But not forever.

He needed a purpose beyond a living sex toy or house boy or tool refurbisher or even staff carpenter.

"Well I'm not sure about that. The rest of the commotion is obviously running behind us some." Morgan edged into the kitchen sniffing the air before she laid a loud, smacking kiss on his cheek. "That smells incredible."

"Thanks." He took his apron off and dug his phone out of his pocket. "I can tell you exactly how much longer they'll be. Hold please."

He tapped an app Devon had installed and took stock of the dots converging on their home. With nine people to keep track of, it was easier if they simply shared their locations with each other. Lately, he'd been using the program to figure out the optimal moment to pop things in the oven.

Morgan peeked over his shoulder.

"Looks like five minutes or less. You have everything under control?" Before he could even be offended, she held up her hands and amended, "Of course you do. Nathan, Klea, Landry, Abby—wash your hands and help Uncle James set the table."

"I've got this. Go wash up, see what the kids did at school today, relax for a bit." James shooed her away. He covered the casserole dish with foil and checked the vegetables he'd roasted to go with the meal before supervising the kids as they set out silverware, glasses, and plates.

People kept trickling in, and soon they were overflowing the massive farmhouse-style dining table. Everyone laughed and shared the highlights or low points of their day. When Mike groused about how he'd stepped in puppy poop, the kids cracked up while his wife, Kate—extra-sensitive to smells in the early part of her pregnancy—scooched her chair closer to Joe instead. He put a familiar hand on her thigh and patted her as he ragged on Mike. Devon plopped down next to James and took his hand, squeezing it as she smiled up at him.

He'd never been part of this kind of family growing up. His had been more likely to holler instead of hoot on the rare occasions they'd actually sat at their wonky dinette table together. Had his own father stepped in shit, he'd have likely kicked their nonexistent dog rather than grumble about the incident. That's if he'd bothered to come home at all. Even worse were the times he hadn't, and James's mom called her brother to watch them while she worked a second job to help them get by. Because on those evenings dread flooded in his sister's eyes. On more than one occasion, she'd been physically ill at the news of their guardian's impending arrival. While he hadn't understood her reaction or her urgent insistence that he stay as far away from their only relative who appeared to give a fuck then, he'd figured it out as he'd gotten older.

If he'd been in her position, he probably would have run away too. But going through the rest of his adolescence alone had been rough. Especially because the bullying set in during high school, after puberty, when it became apparent he wasn't straight or ever going to be big enough to fight back effectively.

So James would never take the family he'd found for granted. Giving Joe and Mike's kids the experiences he'd always dreamed of having when he was their age repaired some of the cracks in his foundation left over from his youth. So much could have been different if he and his sister had the support of even one half-functional adult.

He swallowed hard and looked out the window, wondering as he had a million times before if she was out there somewhere, and if she'd found happiness like he had.

"You okay?" Devon murmured before kissing his cheek.

"Yeah. I'm good." He raised her hand to his lips and bussed her knuckles before Neil swooped in from behind and crushed them both in a monster hug.

"Damn straight you are." Neil laid a smacking kiss on James's mouth, chasing away any lingering malaise before he did the same to Devon. James sighed, feeling secure even if his future wasn't entirely figured out.

He needed the crew. No matter what else was uncertain in his life, this was not.

This was the bedrock he was built on. It kept him from freaking out entirely to know that at least their unwavering support was never going to change.

After they had demolished the entire meatloaf and every bit of the sides—plus an incredible apple cobbler Morgan had brought home from the grand opening of her new bakery, which adjoined Devra's restaurant—the crew pitched in to clean up in record time. They refused to let James help since he'd cooked. Instead he folded his hands over his full stomach and sighed, content, surrounded by people he loved, who miraculously felt the same about him.

They sat around for a while as the younger kids watched something on TV. Abby and Nathan had their heads together as they worked on a graphic novel they were illustrating. The crew talked shop about the various construction sites, the cameras he was going to install the next day, Kayla's business, and Kate's first antique scouting trip with Ollie—the vintage parts sourcer for Hot Rides. Things were falling into place for each of them.

Mike didn't look directly at James when he said, "I ran into Quinn downtown on my way home. He said he tried to snag James for the shop, but he turned them down flat."

"Of course—he's taken. If he's going to be anyone's shop boi, he's mine," Neil teased, not at all upset by the news.

James's guts unknotted a bit. Hopefully they weren't too disappointed in his pickiness. Working with any of the crew, not to mention the Hot Rods or Hot Rides gangs, would be a great gig. Yet here he was passing up opportunities left and right. What the hell was wrong with him?

"I wonder if they offered him more than the Hot Rods. You should have seen those guys drooling over him yesterday," Joe said, attempting to mash Neil's buttons. Hell, maybe all of the crew's. It took a lot to make his husband and wife jealous, but James was willing to be a pawn in Joe's game if it meant it led them to sexy times where they asserted their claim over him and before giving each other happy endings.

Neil's gaze turned possessive. And appreciative. "I don't blame them either. He's sexy and hella talented. What exactly did they want you to do for them? And could we watch?"

"Kids, time to clean up and get ready for bed. We were late getting home tonight and there's school in the morning." Mike crossed his arms, but the look he shot

James and the rest of the crew made it clear none of the adults would be conking out anytime soon.

James wasn't complaining. He needed them and they could tell.

An hour or so later, he paced the floor of the recreation area in the finished basement. It seemed like the kids were finally settled and adult time was on the cusp of beginning.

"I hate seeing you this stressed out," Kayla said from behind him, placing her hands on his shoulders. She stopped him from moving and began rubbing the knots beneath her fingers, putting her massage therapy skills to amazing use.

"Sorry. I don't mean to let my issues spill over to you." James willed himself to relax, but he wasn't able to self-soothe. Failing at even that only made his anxiety worse.

"You were there for me when Bare Natural burned. Let me return the favor. Let us help you work through this, or at least hold your head above water until you figure out how to swim on your own again." Kayla hugged him from behind and he leaned against her.

They were still there, rocking gently, when Devon and Neil rejoined them, having taken showers after their day on their sites. They exchanged a worried glance before cuddling up to either side of his front. Surrounded by them and Kayla, James finally drew a deep breath that put the brakes on the room, which he hadn't even realized was spinning.

The rest of the crew and their wives filed into the space as their duties were done. Joe, the last one in, locked the door behind him in case one of the kids woke up and wandered into forbidden territory. The last thing they wanted to do was traumatize one of them since no kid ever wanted to think of, much less witness their parent getting busy.

"James needs this bad." Dave looked around the room then smiled. "So I guess we'll have to sacrifice and distract him from his worries. I'm pretty sure he can't be a bundle of nerves with all of us focused on trying to relax him."

"I don't want this to be about me." James was tired of everyone looking at him, wondering if he was cracking up or what he would do next. For one night he wanted to be normal again, simply part of the crew, working with them toward a goal. In this case, a sexy one. "Let's make it a ladies' night."

"I'm always down for that." Mike cracked his knuckles.

"Devon's been taking on so much for the crew." James was more impressed by her than ever and he was afraid that his own struggles had meant he hadn't recognized her achievements enough. "Let's show her how much we appreciate her."

"You really have been our MVP lately," Mike agreed. "Shouldering two new projects, helping Kayla with Bare Natural 2, and wrapping things up at the original resort after the fire. Taking charge of our new office space build-out and teaming up with James to keep us all in line as we start off on this new road. You're amazing and we're so lucky you're a Powertool."

"Thank you for saying so." Devon patted James's abs, then slung her arms around Mike's neck before she went on her tiptoes to kiss him sweetly. "But I'm doing this for me, mostly. Let's admit it. We all got comfortable. Things were the same, and great, for so long. It's nice to stretch my wings and show you guys who's really boss."

"Well, I'm always in for that." James perked up. "Go

ahead, take charge. What do you want from me? From us?"

"I mean, I'm not greedy. If it's good enough for the rest of the ladies, it's good enough for me. Besides, you know I like watching them enjoy themselves too. Start with them and work my way." Devon sighed as she looked over Kate, whose hand rested low on her still mostly flat belly, then to Morgan, and finally to her best friend, Kayla.

The past few months had been rough for the women, who'd had their own share of rocky roads to navigate while Kayla grieved for the loss of her original resort in a forest fire and finally accepted Devon's help in reimagining it, even better than before. James knew some of those potholes between them had really jarred Devon, knocking her off kilter. Maybe he could repair whatever lingering misalignment remained.

"I think while we're busy doing that, you and Kayla should amuse each other." James took Kayla's hand from his shoulder and led her to his wife. He pressed it to Devon's cheek, his hand bracketing hers as he dragged it down Devon's neck and collarbone then to her breast.

Both Kayla and Devon sighed.

"This is a great plan." Dave nodded so hard his head was in danger of popping off. He loved watching his wife with Devon, and James couldn't say he minded either. They were so fluid, not exactly gentle but always full of finesse. Watching them was like watching the dirtiest dance he could imagine.

His cock immediately responded, twitching in his pants.

Devon shrugged one shoulder, but James read the relief in her gaze when Kayla leaned in and kissed her, her tongue flickering along Devon's lower lip. She whispered, "They're right, you know? You are incredible. I'm sorry I was too wrapped up in my own drama to tell you so when you were saving my ass. Let me make it up to you."

"There's nothing to forgive." Devon was amazing, because she really meant it. She would do anything for those she loved.

"Oh yeah, there is," Mike rumbled. "I'm sure of it. Lots to say sorry for. Go ahead. Grovel."

Kate snorted, then tapped her husband in his honed gut with the back of her hand. "I'm glad you have someone who will indulge your girl-on-girl fantasies."

"Now all we need is a pillow fight and every one of my teenaged dreams would be realized." Mike never took his eyes off Devon and Kayla, who were inching closer, fully making out.

Devon paused devouring Kayla only long enough to tease them. "Put some of those boners to good use, boys. My friends are waiting and I'm going to be horny as fuck by the time you get to me. You better not disappoint me and come too soon."

"It doesn't exactly help our stamina when you two are being so sexy." Joe didn't try to stop them as he began to strip.

James joined in the flurry of disrobing, flinging his clothes who knew where as he bared himself to the crew and took them in while he was at it. Damn, he was going to have to start exercising if he wasn't working a job site every day. No way was he going to be the only one of them to slack when the rest were covered in thick muscle and contoured bodies. The women were equally as stunning, each of them unique and beautiful in their own ways. None was as compact or almost boyish as Devon. Kate and Morgan fell somewhere in between her and Kayla, who was the tallest and statuesque.

Kate raised her hand somewhat shyly. "Can I be first?"

"Yeah?" Mike whipped his head to her and grinned. "I wasn't sure if you were going to be up for this. I know last time you were pregnant..."

"Maybe at some point I'll be overwhelmed again, but for now I think these hormones are having the opposite effect. I swear I could come just from looking at you guys." She raked her gaze over her husband, Joe, Dave, and Neil. When she got to James it was clear she was hungry for a lot more than his meatloaf.

"Go." Devon smacked James's ass, then returned to Kayla, who apparently made one hell of an appetizer. James looked over his shoulder at the women, who were stripping each other as they ground together, before crossing to Kate.

"I have a feeling I'm the one who's going to lose it quickly this time." She blushed. "Don't laugh too hard if I do, okay?"

"That's not the reaction I'm likely to have to you exploding around us." Mike kissed her temple then guided her to the floor. Most of it was covered with the world's largest mattress they'd rigged up by sewing a few together then covering the bed in a frankensteined futon cover or five. The entirely thing was mounded with pillows and cushions.

It was great for movie nights, and *party* nights too.

By the time Kate was on her back, the five men surrounded her, sinking to their knees. Mike walked her soft pajama pants down her shapely legs before getting rid of the matching top. Her nipples were already rock hard so James didn't hesitate. He leaned in and covered one with his lips, Neil mirroring him on Kate's opposite side. Together they licked and suckled, knowing how sensitive she was ordinarily and how that went double right then.

He didn't have to worry he wasn't useful then because she plunged her fingers into his hair and trapped his face tight to her breast, moaning and arching her back to feed him more of herself.

Mike ran his hands down her belly lovingly as he directed Dave between her legs. "I think you'd better do the honors for me. If we're going to make it through all four of our ladies, I want to last. Besides, you heard the lady, she's horny as hell and you've got the biggest dick."

Kate nibbled on her lower lip and spread her legs to accommodate Dave's bulk.

"Honestly, I need to." Dave kissed Kate, smooshing James and Neil tighter to her with his chest before glancing over at the spot where Kayla and Devon had sunk to the mattress nearby and were stretching out, rocking as they fit themselves together from head to toe. "My balls ache watching them. I have to fuck."

9

———

Kate nodded and reached for his hip, pulling him tight to her core.

Meanwhile, Mike slid behind James and took over where Dave had left off, slipping his tongue into Kate's mouth. If his rock-hard cock rode the furrow of James's ass as they both attended to her, neither of them minded the bonus.

James must have groaned because Neil looked up and winked, encouraging him to take as much pleasure as he could from the crew. Every place they touched was a promise that he belonged and that they would take care of him. That he had a purpose, even if he wasn't sure about where to go next.

Joe fit in beside Neil, his arm going around Neil's waist, anchoring them together as he craned his neck for a taste of Kate. He dragged the tip of his tongue around her mound, accustoming her to his touch before he settled his lips around her clit and began to suck lightly.

Kate moaned into Mike's mouth. Her hips lifted off the floor. Dave took the opportunity to feed her a finger and then a second, making sure she was ready for his impressive cock. He murmured, "Damn, she's soaked."

When she began to tremble beneath them, James realized she hadn't been exaggerating about how much she craved them. She was on the edge. Simply being at the center of the crew, she was already primed and ready to come apart for them. He ran his hands from her shoulder down her arm, hoping to soothe her, but it seemed his touches and those of the rest of the men only inflamed her further.

"Dave, hurry." Her plea was garbled around Mike's kisses, but they understood what she wanted.

Joe put his hands on her mound and spread her for his friend, who notched the fat head of his cock at her opening. James understood full well what that moment of anticipation was like, knowing that Dave's advance might sting a bit but that his gentle strokes and the pleasure he'd impart with his fucking would take away any initial discomfort quickly.

Kate's ribs stopped moving beneath James's fingers, and he warned her, "Keep breathing."

She nodded a bit then did as Dave slid into her. He had to do it in stages, working into her bit by bit, but by the time Kate held all of him inside her, she was quivering and moaning. Joe only amplified the effects when he resumed wriggling his tongue over her clit.

Dave began to move, pumping into her with slow, languid glides that filled her completely without being too rough. And before he'd had a chance to really get going, Kate stiffened. "I'm—"

"We know," Mike promised her with a kiss on her forehead. He stared into his wife's eyes as she unraveled around his crewmate and in the arms of his best friends.

Her orgasm struck fast and hard, rippling through her whole body. James was a little jealous of her release and the intensity of it, which seemed to drain her.

When she went limp between them, they backed off, placing lingering kisses on her flushed skin before turning as one for their next very willing target.

Morgan wiggled her fingers from where she reclined, watching what they'd done to her best friend as well as the show Devon and Kayla were putting on as Devon used the muscles she'd honed on the crew to pin Kayla, who was taller than her but not stronger, to the mattress. Kayla held her own, though, grinding against the thigh Devon planted between her legs, nudging Devon's mound with her other leg.

"Damn, how are you so flexible?" Devon groaned and scissored Kayla back. "Maybe I need to start taking Pilates classes at the spa when it's done. Or practicing yoga with Holden and Sabra like you do."

James reached down and stroked his own cock as he thought of what new talents his wife might develop if she followed through on that threat. She was so beautiful while in charge and simultaneously pleasing herself with her friend. He could have watched the two women for the rest of his life and never gotten bored.

Neil stroked his flank and murmured, "I wonder if this is how she feels when she watches me fuck you."

James shuddered. "If you keep talking like that I'm not going to make it to find out."

Neil chuckled, then raked his teeth over James's neck. "I love you too. Now, help me rock Morgan's world as much as we just did Kate's."

Kate sighed from behind them, her toes flexing as she stretched then curled into a ball, hugging a pillow as she watched the rest of them keep playing. Mike gave her one last tender kiss before she shooed him away. "Go have fun. Come back when you're ready to snuggle."

"Yes, ma'am." He smiled, then turned, stalking toward the place where Joe had settled on top of his wife and was rubbing along her length, getting her ready for their invasion.

The men swarmed her, repeating the process, each of them taking some part of her and doing their damnedest to saturate her with pleasure.

As they ravished Morgan, the moans from Devon and Kayla changed pitch and intensity. James flicked his gaze in their direction in time to see that Devon had swung around and now had her face buried between Kayla's legs. Kayla was reciprocating, making Devon whimper as they went down on each other.

Fuck, that was hot. He rubbed himself against Morgan once or twice before pulling his hips back again. He didn't want to shoot before he was buried inside Devon, locked together in some combination with her and Neil.

"You guys aren't going to be able to resist that for long." Morgan smiled, then beckoned to them. "Someone fuck me so you can join them before they get each other off five or ten times."

As she said it, it seemed that Devon tried to prove her right. The women cried out and clung to each other, shuddering in each other's arms. They loved doing this and seeing how long they could go in a chain of ecstasy that made every one of the guys envious of their ability to orgasm so often.

"Me. It's got to be me." Mike grimaced as he stroked his cock. "Shit. Sorry, first watching Kate and now that..."

"It's a lot." Joe smiled at his friend. "Go ahead. Make my wife come. And hurry up."

He slapped Mike's ass and the foreman, for once, did as he was told.

Mike settled between Morgan's thighs and fit himself to her. When he tried to introduce himself gradually, she hooked a leg around his waist, then screwed her hips upward until she had captured him fully within her.

"It gets me too, you know. Seeing you guys with one of us, helping us live our best life." She glanced over at Kayla and Devon, who rolled, taking turns on top of one another as they brought each other up again.

"Good," Joe told her before kissing the shit out of her. "Because I want you to feel it. This overwhelming desire and the need to let go, to trust the rest of us to catch you. Because we will."

"I know," she whispered before closing her eyes and surrendering to the caresses of ten hands gliding across her skin, Mike's cock deep within her, and the glancing contact from the rest of their hard-ons as they licked, nipped, and caressed her.

James kissed a path down her soft stomach, loving how different it was from the other crewmembers' forms. He rubbed his cheek against her before drawing a long line from Mike's torso, down the base of his cock and then across Morgan's pussy. As Mike fucked, James sucked, flicked, and nuzzled the junction of their bodies.

Both of them seemed to approve. Morgan's cries escalated and the muscles in her quads gathered as she neared her peak.

"Fuck, she's so tight. She's going to come." None of the other guys needed Mike's heads-up. Morgan's body communicated everything they needed to know, encouraging them to increase the intensity of their attention on her. "Neil, I need you to get in here. I won't be able to resist after fucking her."

"Don't stop!" Morgan reached for Mike, but he withdrew. Neil was there in an instant, his cock replacing Mike's as the foreman tapped out.

And though Neil cursed at the ceiling, his eyes clenched shut, he didn't go over the edge when Morgan fell, her pussy attempting to wring him dry.

Mike wiped sweat from his brow with the back of his hand. "That was close."

Morgan whipped her head back and forth as she came all over Neil and in the embrace of the rest of the crew. When they'd eased her down gently, they turned to Kayla and Devon like a pack of ravenous wolves.

"Kayla's next? You're sure?" Mike asked the women.

"I'm too turned on to wait." Devon fished around behind her, her hand landing on James's knee.

"Me too. We can share. There are enough cocks for us both. Come on. Someone fuck us." Kayla didn't have to ask twice. Dave angled onto his side behind her and rocked, his cock seeking entrance before she'd hardly finished her request. Kayla seemed fine with that, eager to get back to licking Devon's pussy. The two women rested on their sides, so Dave and James helped, holding their top knees up to make more room for them all.

Devon tugged on James and he went where she directed, aligning so that he was plastered to her back, his cock tucked between her legs and his face inches from the place where she was still thrilling Kayla. Dave's cock began to sink inside the other woman's pussy. He loved watching it spread the other woman from so close up. It reminded him of the weekend he and James had spent in her cabin with Dave, snowed in, at the beginning of their relationship.

Neil reached between James's legs from behind and steered James's cock to their wife while his own hands were too occupied by holding her knee and bracing himself to do it himself. "Go on, James. Give her what she's asking for."

"And you?" James asked, licking his lips. He'd be happy to suck Neil as he fucked their wife. He was plenty capable of doing two things at once.

"Not tonight." Neil rubbed his thumb over James's mouth and smiled. "I want to be inside you. For us all to be united. For you to know that your place is here, with us. And none of this other shit freaking you out changes that. Understand?"

James nodded even as he looked past Devon and Kayla and Dave to Mike, who was doing the same. He and Joe knelt, Mike near James's head and Joe behind Dave. Their fists pumped their cocks in time to the bobbing of Devon and Kayla's heads.

Kate and Morgan edged closer, running their hands over their husband's backs and asses and whatever else they could reach. They urged them on, telling them how sexy they were and how they'd earned their releases. Morgan egged Joe on. "I've got some lube right here. Maybe you should fuck Dave so that he explodes. You know how turned on he gets when he watches Kayla and Devon together."

"Yes. Yes." Kayla wasn't capable of more than chanting against Devon's slick flesh.

James grunted when Neil slapped his ass. "Hurry up, Joe. I need that too and I'm not real patient right now."

Joe laughed as he slathered his cock then tossed the lube to Neil.

James kissed Devon's neck and drew in a deep breath, loving the sweet musk of Kayla's arousal. He pressed forward, his cock boring into his wife even as Neil quickly coated himself and touched his slick cock to James's ass.

He was stuck, pinned in place by Devon and Neil, only able to give and take as they allowed. It was heaven. He didn't have to think. Didn't have to worry. Didn't have to second guess, because this was his zone, where he was meant to be and where he would always belong.

It was only more evident when Mike fisted James's hair and steered his mouth toward Mike's cock. He opened his mouth, his neck straining so that he could swallow the foreman whole. Buried in Devon, James took all of Neil and Mike too. Meanwhile, Dave tunneled into Kayla as Devon licked his wife's clit and Joe fit himself into Dave's ass.

James swallowed around Mike, making the man groan. Kate whispered words of encouragement to him, telling him how this was only possible because of the crew he'd built and his leadership, which had encouraged each of them to embrace what they needed, even if it was unconventional. She ran her hands down his arms from behind, then up his abs and over his chest, pausing to thumb his tight nipples.

James tasted the first spurt of Mike's precome as Neil began to ride, fucking James's ass and causing him to pound into Devon equally as hard. His wife moaned, then arched into his hold as Kayla did the same to Dave. The big guy cursed when Joe's hips began to slap against Dave's ass, his lunges losing some of their control in favor of raw passion.

And that's when James began to float.

In that state where none of them was bound by conscious thought and simply acted, where he wished they could exist forever, though it never lasted quite long enough to keep him from wanting to do it again and again.

Everyone surrounded him, Devon, and Kayla.

They ran their hands through the women's hair, over their arms, the side of their breasts, the dip of her waists. Neil added his hand to James's, raising her knee higher, spreading her even more for James's penetration. He fused himself to her, every inch of his skin that touched her singing with the contact.

James clung to her, relying on Neil to drive him into her with the force of his plunges, which became faster and jerkier with time. Kayla howled against Devon's pussy as Dave fucked her, burying fully between her legs as Joe bottomed out in his ass.

James closed his eyes and tried to hang on, but the need to fly and give them everything he had nearly overwhelmed his restraint. Passion whipped around him like wind in a hurricane. And soon he wasn't the only one clinging to self-control by his fingernails.

"Fuck. Fuck!" Mike growled as James sucked harder, swirling his tongue around the head of their foreman's cock.

"I am." Joe groaned. "But not for long."

"Is everyone ready?" Mike asked.

It wasn't often they all came together, but this was one of those magical moments. James could feel it. Each of them had been afraid, in their own way, of this massive move and the change to their lives, which had been amazing before and would be even better now.

It was relief propelling them, and excitement. For the future. For what they were building together, even if it wasn't in the same way as before.

"Going. Now," Devon panted before she writhed in his arms. Her pussy smothered his cock even as he crashed into her, spilling deep within her as Neil did the same. He flooded James's ass as he roared, his teeth sinking into James's shoulder while he held James tight.

Then James was swallowing as fast as he could to keep up with the pumping of Mike's cock in his throat. But even he couldn't keep up and a few drops spilled from the corner of his mouth as he shuddered and drained himself into Devon.

Dave's balls were drawn tight to his body and pulsing in front of James's face as he unloaded into Kayla, and Joe was drawn by the clamp of Dave's ass on his cock into a stellar orgasm of his own.

For a minute it was as if every molecule of oxygen was sucked from the room. They were still and quiet. And when they relaxed, moaning, groaning, and disentangling themselves, it wasn't to go far.

The crew snuggled, a pile of tangled limbs and shared partners. James took a deep breath for the first time in what seemed like forever. Then another and another.

He helped Devon twist around so they were face to face then hugged her tight to him, while Neil did the same to him from behind. "It's going to be okay, James. You'll figure this out. And until then, we've got you."

James ignored the stinging in his eyes and nodded sharply. Because he knew it was true and he'd never been so damn grateful for the crew as he was at that moment.

10

———

Usually after a session with the crew like the one they'd indulged in the night before, James would be floating around on a euphoric high that would last for days afterward. This time, not so much.

Neil cursed from the closet, making James grumble, "If you'd hang your clothes up when you took them out of the damn dryer you would know where they were when you needed to get dressed."

"Sorry. Sorry." Neil hopped on one foot as he dragged his jeans up his defined legs. "I'll try to be more like you. You probably know where that fugly light-up sweater we made for the Christmas contest ten years ago is."

"Second shelf, all the way to the back left." Damn straight he did. He wasn't a master organizer for nothing.

"I didn't mean to wake you up." Neil came closer, wincing. "You should sleep in. Catch up on your rest. No need to get up if you don't have to be somewhere, even if I do miss my breakfast sandwich."

Devon smacked Neil's ass for James. But somehow even that didn't make him smile.

"For the record, I *do* actually have something to do." James cursed. "I told Jordan I'd install those security cameras on our sites, starting with Devon's. The equipment has probably been sitting on the porch longer than is wise. Hopefully, it didn't get stolen. That would be an awesome way to prove I'm not worthless."

"Hey." Neil shot him a concerned glance. "Stop talking about yourself like that or I'm going to get irritable too."

"We probably don't even need—"

"You're getting them so don't waste your breath." James sliced his hands through the air.

"Fine, but don't worry. I heard Joe take the puppy out at the ass crack of dawn and then some thuds so I'm sure he brought the gear in for you already."

"And now Joe's covering for me too? Great."

"Uh oh. This is a serious case of the grumpies." Devon paused and sat on the edge of the bed. When she reached for James's hand, he levered himself up, brushing her fingers away. He had to take a shower, get dressed, and go to work making his lovers safer.

"No, it's not. I'm annoyed with myself. I need to get my shit together. I'm the only one who can fix whatever the hell is wrong with me. Except I fucking can't seem to pull my head out of my ass." James threw up his hands, wishing he could figure out how to untangle the knot of worry and grief and indecision that had been choking him from the inside out for weeks. Now he wasn't even pulling his weight around the house. His husband was going to go to work hungry and James was going to be the one late to a job site.

Okay, so it was more likely that Neil would swing by the drive thru and chow down on a couple of those greasy hash brown patties he loved, but that didn't make James feel less guilty.

"I see." Devon didn't curse him out for being an asshole or flinch at his dramatic gesture, but he could tell by the way her face turned stony that he'd hurt her feelings.

"Shit. I'm sorry." He reached for her. Neil came near too. He plopped onto the bed and huddled up with them both. Before James could beg forgiveness for his foul mood, his phone started buzzing on the nightstand.

When he saw *Tom* lighting up the screen, he grabbed it. Why would the patriarch of the Hot Rods and Hot Rides gangs call him this early?

After exchanging a worried glance with Devon and Neil, James answered on speakerphone, "Hey, Tom. What's up?"

"You apparently." Tom snorted at his dad joke. "I hope I didn't wake you, but I need a favor and I think you're the right man for the job."

"Morning, Tom," Neil said so the guy—Eli's father and Joe's uncle—would know he was talking to an audience. "Apparently everyone in Middletown has a use for my man today."

Devon smiled at James. "He *is* pretty handy."

James couldn't help but smirk back, his ire dissipating a bit. These two and the rest of the crew sure were good for a man's ego. Before Tom could read too much into their comments, James asked, "What can I do for you?"

"Feel free to say no. But...you know the shelter my first wife founded in town for at-risk youth?" Tom didn't talk about the place very much, but James knew it was incredibly important to him even though it was laced with bittersweet memories.

"The one where you found those ragamuffin Hot Rods and brought them home from?" James teased. "Yeah, of course. What about it?"

"Well, it seems they're shorthanded. They need a shop teacher to work with a special student. I told our director, Ms. Rodriguez, that I might know someone qualified to fill in for a bit. Would you mind going down there and lending a hand this afternoon?"

James clenched his eyes shut so he didn't have to witness the genuine curiosity in Neil and Devon's gazes. His heart started beating faster and his palms got sweaty in a flash. The youth shelter? That could be an incredibly worthwhile place to invest his time. Working with kids would definitely be more inspirational than the other options he'd come up with so far. Something like enthusiasm rose in him until his better sense squashed it. "Uh, I don't know, Tom. I'm not sure I'm exactly a good role model for an impressionable young person."

"What the fuck are you talking about?" Neil reared up, making James's eyes fly open.

Devon was staring at him with her head tipped as if he was stupid. "Of course you are, James."

"You're perfect for this. Trust me." Tom didn't stop there. "Uh, the kid is gay and has been teased a bunch. To the point that our director is concerned he might turn to self-harm. He could learn a lot from you about how to appreciate himself even when others might not."

Tom's well-thought-out logic made James wonder exactly how long he'd been cooking up this so-called last minute request.

Neil clenched James's hand. "You should do it. You're strong. You dealt with plenty of bullies when you were his age and unlike most other guys in your class. I bet there's lots of kids out there, not only the one Tom is reaching out about, who could really benefit from hearing that message from you."

"Especially if you can encourage them and promise them there's someone or someones waiting to love them as much as we love you so they hang on long enough to find them." Devon nodded.

James reminded himself that although he didn't know what his future held, he never once doubted this part of his life. He was so damn fortunate. They were right—it would be selfish of him to keep that information to himself. Wrong *not* to give back.

Besides, what the hell else was he going to do after finishing the surveillance install except lie on the couch and doom scroll on his phone all day? Maybe peek in at the nosy neighbor group and gossip about the police scanner some more? Not likely.

"You said you wanted to do something meaningful. What could matter more than this?" Devon rubbed his arm. "I don't know where I'd be if I didn't have you. Go, James. Make a difference in this kid's world and his future-Devon or future-Neil will have you to thank, even if they never know it."

Neil looped his arm around James's shoulders. "You got this."

"Listen to your wife and your husband. They're smart," Tom prodded. "And honestly, I'm not sure who else to ask. I'm in a bind. Please?"

That was a knee straight to the balls.

Tom didn't ask for favors very often. Hell, James couldn't remember the guy ever making a request despite being there to save their asses or kick them, whenever he was needed. "Yeah, okay. I'll do it. I hope you all are right and I don't make things harder for this kid somehow. Hanging out with me isn't likely to be a point in his favor with the assholes picking on him."

"He can handle himself, like you learned to do. He just needs someone to point him in the right direction." Tom seemed awfully smug.

"I never was a Boy Scout. But you're right, I made it through those hellish years and I can maybe teach this kid a few survival skills. Or at least how to measure twice and cut once. Equally valuable life lessons, I guess."

Neil laughed and Devon kissed his cheek.

"I need to set up some cameras on the crew sites for Jordan first. Is that okay?"

"Oh, yeah!" Tom seemed really interested. "That's a great idea, actually. I thought about mentioning it to him but I know he's...busy...this week."

"So I heard. That's why I volunteered. I should be able to figure this out." At least he hoped he wouldn't have to bug the guy much. "What time do they need me there?"

"Around two. Will that work?"

James nabbed his planner off the side table, flipped it open and confirmed his yawning page of nothingness before penciling in both the security job and then the shelter appointment. Wow, two whole things in one day. That made him a little more eager to get rolling anyway. "It should. I can always finish the install job afterward."

"Perfect. Let me know how it goes, kid." Tom hung up and James sat, staring at the phone in his hand. Something about being called *kid*, as if Tom wouldn't mind if James had been his own flesh and blood, did funny things to his insides.

Tom was a good man. The confidence he had in James might have had something to do with the warm fuzzies floating around in his guts too. His glower evaporated, replaced by a tentative smile.

If nothing else, James didn't want to let down Tom, who was the closest thing he had to a true dad or Jordan, who was giving him the tools to look after the crew.

"Guess you better hit the shower and get dressed." Neil kissed James, then gave him a tight hug.

Devon nodded and took her turn. "You're going to do great today."

James wasn't as confident as either of his spouses, but he did trust them with everything he had, including his soul, so he opted to believe they were right.

11

———

James was whistling by the time he hauled the first batch of equipment from the hatch-back of his snazzy, good-as-new-again car and carried it to the clearing where Devon was overseeing the pouring of the spa foundation. He saluted her but didn't interrupt, instead heading toward the temporary utility pole where their electricity was run for the site.

He sat cross-legged on the ground and sliced open the box with his pocket knife before removing a packet of instructions. Unlike Neil, who would have tossed them aside in favor of figuring it out himself, James thoroughly read every word before beginning.

The installation itself was going to be a piece of cake, but the networking aspect of it was new to him. Good thing he'd brought his laptop, and his planner—of course—in his backpack.

He unpacked the cameras, wires, transmitters, and mounting plates, inventorying all of the components before opening his travel tool-kit. Everything inside was laid out in orderly rows, precisely where he had put it.

It took less than thirty minutes before he'd knocked out the physical connections and had the system humming away and displaying an image of the entire site on his screen. At that point, he picked up his cell and dialed Jordan.

"How's it going?" Jordan answered without bothering with hello.

"Good. Sorry to interrupt, I know you're busy, but I'm ready to establish the network connections whenever you have a moment. Either now or I can come back whenever…"

"This is fine." Jordan was terse but kind. James could work with that. He shut down his natural chatty tendencies and focused on just the facts. "I'm going to hand you off to Sola, who's the head of our tech and comms team. When you're finished with her, come back to me for a wrap up."

"Will do." James leaned in, Jordan's focus rubbing off on him. He would have been lying if he said he didn't feed off their sense of urgency. Plus, it fired him up that he was capable enough to handle the stuff on his end with minimal direction. It was like the feeling he got when he coordinated complicated processes, like insurance bullshit, for the crew and helped make their lives just a little easier.

"Hey, there." A woman came on the line. She shared Jordan's rapid, to-the-point style.

"Hi. I think I have the cameras all set up and broadcasting. What's next?"

"First I'll need you to look up the IP addresses for each device. Open the control panel, then click…"

James followed her step by step instructions, allowing her to drive his hands as they flew over the keyboard, entered commands, and clicked through menus he'd never seen before. In less than five minutes, they'd done it.

"Aha. I see you now." She laughed when he blew her a kiss over the camera feed. "And more importantly, I see the entire construction site. Is that woman over there your wife?"

"Yup." James puffed up with more pride than he'd felt at nailing the camera install.

"She's cute. And badass. Look at her bossing around all those construction workers."

"Yes, she is." He nodded, beaming at Devon. "She's a great foreman."

"I'm sure she is. And now we'll make sure there's no funny business going on to derail her projects. You think you'll remember how to link the system at the other sites?"

James peeked down at the neat, precise instructions he'd written in the dot grid section of his planner. "Pretty sure."

"If you get stuck, call back." Sola handed him off to Jordan. "Hey, Boss, I'm putting James back on your line. And I take back my bitching from before... He doesn't suck for a regular civilian. In fact, I give him an A+."

Jordan came back. "Ah, sorry about that. Sola—"

"Doesn't take any shit. I like it." James grinned. "Thanks for the gear and the help connecting it to your system. We really appreciate you guys monitoring the feeds and making sure everything is on the up and up here."

"It's no problem."

"Do you think there's something to worry about?" James wondered.

"Not super likely. Middletown is pretty sedate. But it

never hurts to be cautious. I've seen enough in my career to never take things for granted."

"I bet. And on that note, I'll let you get back to saving the world." He couldn't prevent just a little of his curiosity from spilling out first, though. "That is what you do, right? Do you have a whole team up there in your mountain mansion? And a command center or headquarters where there are all sorts of feeds coming in or what?"

"I could tell you, but then I'd have to kill you," Jordan deadpanned.

"Was that a joke?" The more James thought about it, the more fascinated he was even knowing he should let it go.

Jordan simply laughed. "Yeah. Now go wire the rest of the sites. I'll text you Sola's direct number. Work with her if you need something during the process then send me a status update when you're finished and we're all set to go."

"Will do." James channeled his inner super spy. He could get into this.

"But for the record, I honestly believe we're the good guys even if we sometimes have to stop people who aren't."

"That makes sense." James knew Jordan had previously worked for the government and could imagine situations where knowing what was right didn't mean you could do anything about it given the restrictions of your position. That would totally suck.

In the background, a man called for Jordan's attention. "I've got to go. Good job."

James sat there for a moment, staring at his disconnected phone. For the first time in a while, he felt like he might just have done something right and something kind of important at the same time. It was a satisfying combo.

With a wave to Devon, he strutted to his car then zoomed off to the next site, determined to reduce his install time at each location and only bug Sola for long enough to confirm each camera was functioning correctly before moving on to the next.

12

James had knocked out the surveillance installation in record time, or so Jordan had promised him in an impressed-sounding text. That had left him two hours to go home, eat lunch, take a shower, and get changed before he had to leave for the youth center.

His lingering confidence propelled him through those tasks and kept him from freaking out until he'd reached the parking lot of the youth center. Then, as he considered what faith Tom had put in him, James's palms began to sweat. He wondered how much Tom would hate him if he backed out at the last second.

James wasn't about to risk it, so he put on his big-boy panties and scooted out of his car pretending to be as brave as his idol, Robin, when he identified a hell of lot more with his alter-ego Dick Grayson.

James tugged on his plaid work shirt, which he'd buttoned up and tucked in as if that made him respectable or professionally dressed. He glanced around as he walked through the front door, then headed toward the back to the director's office, as he'd been instructed in a text from Tom.

As he wandered through the facilities, he noticed most people were far more casual than him, trying to blend in with the kids who might not own much more than a well-worn pair of jeans and sneakers with a few holes in them.

Suddenly he felt like an idiot. This was about helping others, not boosting his own flagging self-esteem. And furthermore, he wanted to relate, not stick out.

He stopped in front of a window that looked onto a basketball court long enough to mess his hair up from the slicked-back style he'd combed it into after his shower. He untucked his shirt and opened the buttons so it hung open, exposing the white T-shirt beneath it. Better.

James took a deep breath, wiped his palms on his pants, then crossed to an open doorway in the general vicinity Tom had indicated. He knocked lightly on the jamb, then peeked inside where a woman a few years older than him sat, dressed in a T-shirt with the shelter's logo on it. Her dark hair fell in natural waves around her face, and she smiled warmly before he could even start speaking.

"Good morning. I'm looking for Ms. Rodriguez."

"That's me. You must be James." She waved toward one of the comfy chairs around her desk. He could tell she was good at her job, since even his nervous self settled in easily. The open and inviting atmosphere she established made him feel like he was pulling up a chair at a café to catch up with an old friend instead of being interviewed by a superior.

"Thanks for taking time to get me up to speed this afternoon. I heard you're shorthanded as it is."

"You're welcome. We're always glad to have more helping hands and kind ears around this place. Tom told me you're interested in working with kids who've been bullied or are struggling with their sexuality."

Well, that wasn't exactly how it had gone down, but... "Those are certainly two areas I have experience in."

"I'm sorry to hear that." She leaned forward and stared straight into his eyes. Bronze flecks shot through the deeper brown of her pupils, but that wasn't the most remarkable thing about her stare. It was the kindness emanating from her that made him sure she cared about him as much as any other lost soul who walked through the doors of the youth shelter.

The same place that had been responsible for getting each of the Hot Rods off the streets and into a loving home where they had also discovered and bonded with each other. For a moment James wondered if Laurel could have been so lucky.

He cleared his throat, surprised by the jolt thinking of his long-lost sister could deliver even now, more than twenty-five years after she'd bailed on him. The ball of anger, dread, and sadness that encompassed his feelings about her bounced around his guts for a moment until Ms. Rodriguez interrupted his meandering thoughts.

"There's a boy out in the workshop. He's come in once or twice before, but usually to pick up a bag lunch. Yesterday was the first day he accepted our offer to stay for a while, and our counselors were...concerned. He's showing an interest in the shop area. You are a construction worker, yes?"

"I was." James cleared his throat. It seemed odd to think of it as a closed chapter of his life. "For more than twenty years."

"Maybe you could teach him something about tools or see if there's something he needs or wants to make. That part isn't as important as spending time with him and maybe helping him realize that whatever he's facing now is temporary. Tom was right. This seems like a perfect match to me." Ms. Rodriguez smiled at James. "You'll do great. Just be yourself. Most of these kids really only need a normal person to talk to."

"Well, he's probably screwed then. I've never been accused of being *normal* before." James rolled his eyes.

Her smile only grew. "Fair point. Let me rephrase. Most of these kids need a kind, open-minded, rational adult to show them that the examples they've had so far in life are not what they should expect going forward."

Right. Just like the Powertools had demonstrated to him how dysfunctional his own family had been. "Okay. I think I can pull that off."

"I'm sure you can. The workshop is down the hall, second door on the left. Feel free to use anything you find in there, and we're open to any and all suggestions about how we can improve it. Tom told me you're extremely good at carpentry, even if you're modest. And Tom is a tough man to impress."

"Thank you." When James rose, he found his muscles were no longer bunched and he was actually looking forward to what he might be able to bring to the table saw, so to speak.

"Let me know if there's anything you need." The open-endedness of her statement gave James the impression that she wasn't only talking about his assignment. He hoped Tom paid her as much as he could afford. She was worth it.

When James entered the shop, he identified the boy Ms. Rodriguez had been referring to without having to ask. Okay, he was the only person in there, slouched on a stool, inspecting the various stations from a distance. Still, the kid could have been a mirror reflection of James at that age, or maybe the ghost of the preteen who still haunted him from somewhere deep down in his subconscious.

At the sound of the metal door shutting, the kid's eyes flashed around the room as if he expected someone to jump him. He'd gathered his backpack and the bag lunch provided by the shelter together and piled them on top of each other, between his legs, to keep anyone from stealing them.

He had not one ounce of trust to spare.

James waved as he approached slowly and kept his voice low. Thank God Tom had sent him and not one of the other, bulkier crew guys. Dave, although he was a gentle giant, would have probably made this kid piss his pants. "Hi, I'm James."

The mop of unruly brown hair covered most of the kid's eyes as he peered up and said, "Hey. I'm Mark."

"Nice to meet you." James checked out the workshop, which was no grungy, dusty hole in the wall. It was bright and recently painted with gently used, almost top-of-the-line equipment. Very nice. "This place is pretty sweet. It's my first day here."

"Really? Mine too, kind of." Mark's shoulders seemed to relax a bit.

"Yeah. I just moved to Middletown a few weeks ago."

"Sorry. I'd give anything to get the hell out of here."

James smiled sadly at that. "I remember feeling the

same way when I was your age. But I guess I've learned that a place is mostly what you make of it. There's nowhere you can go to escape yourself, and if you're happy with who you are, you can do okay pretty much anywhere."

"Hmm." Mark didn't sound convinced. That was okay—James didn't blame him for doubting.

"So...did you have something in mind you wanted to build today? Or anything you'd like to learn about? I've worked in construction for, well, probably longer than you've been alive. Which makes me feel like an old fart."

Mark laughed, and James thought he might have already won the day with that feat. "I, uh, wasn't really thinking of anything specific. I just want to figure out how to do stuff that could maybe get me a job sometime. Maybe soon?" He seemed afraid to hope.

"Yeah, I could definitely help you with that. How old are you, anyway?"

"Fourteen."

"Ah, I remember those days of constant wedgies from jerks at school and never feeling comfortable in my own skin."

"Sucks." The kid grimaced.

"Well, it gets better. I promise you that." James realized it was true. He couldn't even remember the last time he'd been made to feel awkward about being bisexual—although back then he probably would have said he was gay if someone asked—or poly or short or, well, anything really. That made him pause for a second then smile. He might not know exactly where he was going, but he sure had come a long way.

"All right. So, first let's spend some time learning

about safety and measuring. Then we can practice ripping some boards on the table saw before you get to experience the joys of sweeping up sawdust."

Mark snorted and took the pair of safety glasses James handed him. After James had bored Mark with fractions, warnings about how easy it was to lose a finger, and the old *measure twice, cut once* adage, which gave the illusion that he was wise, he demonstrated how to set the fence and use a push stick instead of a bare hand to feed boards over the blade.

Mark had a keen eye, keeping the board tight to the fence when it tended to wander, and never once made James lunge for the kill switch. He soaked up information quick and had a natural talent for shop work. The time whizzed past as fast as the power tools, and pretty soon they'd whipped out a birdhouse.

"Come again tomorrow and you can paint it and install it out back, unless you have somewhere you'd like to put it at home. Maybe watching the birds would take your mind off things there when they're not going so good," James suggested, feeling lame because he couldn't offer more.

"Wait, don't you mean *we*? Or are you not working tomorrow?" Mark looked away, but not before James caught the disappointment in his gaze. Oh, damn.

"I'm not sure. I mean, I'm not actually staff here. I only stopped in today to help out a friend and..." Why? Why exactly had he come? It felt really unappreciative to say that he was searching for a new job because he wasn't happy doing an honest day's labor at Powertools, Hot Rods, or Hot Rides when he had all the things he thought he'd never find when he'd been Mark's age. This, like the work he'd done for Jordan earlier, felt like he might be taking some baby steps in the right direction, though. "I guess I'm trying to figure out what to do with myself now that I'm here. My husband and wife have careers in construction. They're working on the tourist center downtown and the new resort going up behind Hot Rods."

"Wait. Did you say husband?" Mark tipped his head. "*And* wife? Is that a thing?"

"Anything is possible in life, I guess." James sighed. "I'm a lucky guy."

"Huh." Mark was quiet for a moment, then nodded. "That's really cool."

"It is. And when I was in your place, I never would have believed it was possible to find one person, never mind two, who love me exactly as I am." James smiled, still half-wondering if it could be a dream.

"Huh." Mark's eyes opened wider and he drew in a deep breath.

James beamed. "You'll find your people someday. You just have to keep looking. Hell, I have a whole crew of friends now. And until then, you know, you've got skills. You could do great at this with a little practice."

"Really?" Mark whipped his head up, his shaggy hair falling out of his face fully for the first time. He blasted James with a gaze so full of longing that it hit him square in the chest.

"Absolutely. If you want, I could talk to my crew about hiring you. I'll have to check the rules and stuff but I'm pretty sure even at this age you'd be okayed to do crap jobs like sweeping up while they show you the ropes and get you trained to take on bigger tasks when it's time. Kind of like an apprentice. What do you think?"

"I would love that, except..."

"Hmm?" James cocked his head.

"I've been thinking about maybe not sticking around Middletown much longer. I don't want to waste anymore of my life here, especially not if *my people* are really out there waiting for me to find them." Mark stared wistfully out the window.

"Are you talking about running away?" James's heart kicked in triple time.

"Yeah. Not that anyone would notice I was gone."

"They would. I'm *sure* that they would." He could hardly breathe. He remembered what it had been like, watching their driveway day after day, year after year, praying he'd catch a glimpse of Laurel coming back home.

He never had.

"Okay, you're right. They would and they'd be glad." Mark looked away, but not fast enough for James to catch the sheen of unshed tears in his stormy gray-blue eyes.

His instincts and every bit of him that had mourned losing his sister so young wanted to argue, but then he had to take a deep breath and consider reality. The Hot Rods had come here and made something new for themselves, a better life. Only Mark really knew if the situation he was in was unbearably toxic and unhealthy. James couldn't afford to fuck this up because of his own bullshit history and twisted feelings, which could easily trip him up, getting in the way of doing the right thing for Mark.

"I'm sorry you don't have the support you should." James chose his words carefully even though he wished he could simply crush the kid in a bear hug and promise him everything would be fine someday. "If you need a place to stay, you should talk to Ms. Rodriguez. There are resources out there. People whose job it is to help you find shelter if that isn't available to you at home. But please, don't take off on your own. It's not safe, and even if no one else in this town would care about what happens to you, *I* would. I can tell after hanging out with you just for a few hours that you're awesome. Don't let shitty circumstances convince you of anything else. You can't control where you start out, but you determine where you end up, and I know you're going to do great things. You have to do it the proper way in order to make sure you get where you're meant to be."

Mark's breath hitched. He looked up at James with wide eyes and a single tear spilled down his cheek, breaking James's heart.

"I've only just met you, but I can tell you're a great kid. Fuck anyone who says otherwise." James figured he probably wasn't supposed to drop the F-bomb around kids, but it was the truth.

"Thanks." The corner of Mark's mouth kicked up in the hint of a smile and he wiped his face on the back of his too-short sleeve. "So, tomorrow...?"

The instinctive flare of emotions Mark had unwittingly triggered when he'd spoken of running away made it clear James wasn't going to be a good fit for the center long term, and probably couldn't be trusted to be unbiased even for a day or two.

"I don't think I'll be here. But I'm going to give you my email and the contact info for the Powertools office. I'll put in a good word with the owners tonight, okay?" James hoped it was enough.

"Yeah. That's great. Thank you so much." Mark carefully folded the piece of paper with the information and tucked it into a zippered pocket on his backpack before patting the outside of it. "Maybe you're right. Maybe things can be different if I'm patient enough."

James walked Mark out to one of the staff counselors and waved goodbye before heading back to Ms. Rodriguez's office. His gut said their paths would cross again. Just not here.

Ms. Rodriguez reclined in her chair, her hands laced over her softly rounded stomach. "I saw the way Mark was looking at you and chatting so freely when you walked past. I've never seen that boy smile before and when I peeked in after you'd been in there less than an hour he was outright laughing at whatever you two were up to. Been here one day and you've already saved somebody. Thank you."

James laughed and held his hands up. "I don't know about all of that, but Mark is great and I'm glad I got to meet him. He taught me a thing or two. Reminded me what's important, you know?"

"I have no idea how Tom manages to find all of you, but...you're just like the rest of his gang, you know that?"

James couldn't have been more complimented. "Thanks. Eli, the Hot Rods, and the Hot Rides are incredible people. They've been through so much and are stronger for it. It's really inspiring."

She nodded. "So, Tom was right as always. He told me you'd fit right in here and after this afternoon, I believe him. Not that I didn't before, but I like to see things for myself when it comes to the kids here. They've been let down enough by life as it is. Anyway, we have an open counselor position. You in?"

"Oh, wow. I don't think I'm qualified for that. Don't you need a degree or a certification at least?"

"Ah, it's not that kind of counselor. Think camp counselor, not psychologist."

"Oh, right. Well, thank you for even considering me. I'm glad I was here today, but no. I'm not ready for this." James realized his history wouldn't work to his or the kids' benefit at the center. "I went through some things in my past—not the bullying and stuff—that I need to work through before I think I could be unbiased enough to work here."

He cleared his throat. Ms. Rodriguez simply waited patiently. Though he didn't mean to spill his guts, she had perfected her tell-me-everything gaze.

"I was seven when my sister disappeared. The police say she ran away from home." Why had he said it that way? Maybe because even after all this time there was part of him that couldn't believe it was true, that she'd willfully abandoned him. "I don't think I could be completely impartial about another situation like that."

"Ah, I see." Ms. Rodriguez still didn't pressure him. But the hurt had been bubbling up at odd times lately, so James figured he should take the chance to talk about Laurel while it was somewhat appropriate and relevant.

"No one ever found her and she never came back. I don't blame her. I suspect she was being abused by our uncle, though I didn't realize it at the time. Still, I have no idea what happened to her. I like to believe she's happy. Out there. Somewhere." Even if it meant she'd never looked back or bothered to reconnect with him.

"Have you ever searched for her as an adult?" Ms. Rodriguez wondered.

"To be honest, for a long time I think I was pissed off at her. A couple years ago, though, I did one of those DNA test thingies and left my info available online for relative matches. And I've poked around on the internet from time to time, but no one with her name has social media profiles that match her as far as I can tell."

"Well, if she was successful in starting over somewhere else, it's likely she changed her name." Ms. Rodriguez sighed. "It's best to stay positive. Maybe she found someplace like our shelter or Tom's garage. Maybe she wasn't out on the streets long, if at all."

"Yeah." James couldn't say he really believed that, but it was a nice thought. "Anyway, I'm sure, given my situation, that I'm not the best match for the center. But if it's okay, I'd like to talk to my friends about giving Mark a job, maybe even an apprenticeship, if that's allowed."

"That would be wonderful, thank you. We're always grateful for opportunities people make available to our kids." Ms. Rodriguez sighed. "If you change your mind about the position, you know where to find us. And if you'd ever like to volunteer for one of our events or clean up days or whatever, I'd love to meet the rest of your family."

"Thank you." It still warmed James to be accepted and welcomed like that, so unconditionally, and so he was sure that for Mark, it could be life changing.

"Do be sure to tell Tom that I tried my hardest to recruit you. He was quite insistent that you'd be a perfect fit for us." She chuckled as she waved him out.

"I'll put in a good word, don't worry. And sorry I couldn't do more."

"You did plenty. Thank you."

At least the day hadn't been a complete bust. Between the camera installations and his time at the shelter, he'd achieved something he'd been trying to accomplish for a while. He felt like he'd done things that mattered. And although the counselor thing hadn't ultimately worked out, he was pretty sure Tom had pointed him in the right direction.

James couldn't wait to talk to Devon, Neil, and Tom about what other opportunities he might find to make a positive difference in someone's life. Because this...this was *almost* what he wanted to do for the rest of his own.

13

"So, yeah, while it was a great day and I really appreciate you vouching for me, it's not going to work out permanently." James met Tom and Ms. Brown's understanding gazes from across their kitchen table. He'd come to explain personally what had happened. He also valued their feedback, which was priceless, about where he might look next. "It did help me narrow things down though."

"That's great, honey." Ms. Brown smiled and placed a blue-and-white plate stacked with fresh cookies on the table in front of him. They were warm and gooey and he couldn't resist. She took a seat next to Tom and said, "So, what have you come up with?"

James opened his planner and flipped to the notes section where he'd brainstormed with the crew the night before. "Okay, so... I like the way it felt when I was doing things for a greater cause. Now I just have to figure out where I can help the most based on what I know how to do."

Tom nodded. "Tell us what you think you're best at; maybe we can help."

"Here are skills we identified last night. I'm hyper-organized, good at building stuff, and could pretty easily expand that knowledge into working with electronics based on the work I did for Jordan yesterday."

"That's a good start. What else do you have on that list of yours?" Ms. Brown tried to peek as she took a cookie for herself from the plate and began to nibble on it.

"Well, Joe and Mike think I'm the best of our guys at staying cool under pressure, which is something I never considered before. But it is true that when they lose their tempers and curse and stomp, I'm usually the one that steps in to cool things down."

"I could see that." Tom stole a bite of Ms. Brown's cookie, making her laugh. "Eli and Joe did always run a little hot."

"Well, it's no secret I'm not like most guys." James grinned, that fact no longer bothering him as much as it used to. "In fact, the Powertools ladies say I'm empathetic, a good listener, and great at communicating. A lot of times they come to me to hash things out before working through a problem with their spouses and making sure they can deal with issues in an effective way."

"Now *that* is a rare talent." Ms. Brown patted his hand.

"Anything else?" Tom wondered.

"Just a couple odds and ends. For example, I'm not afraid of working hard. And I'm open-minded. Hell, we're all obviously fine with being unconventional if it's for a good cause. And I have some computer skills, but I guess everyone does these days."

Tom huffed and shook his head. "Not me so much. Sure, I can check my email but I swear Holden and Sabra's twins can run circles around me on my phone or that laptop Eli got me last Christmas."

James snatched another cookie and demolished it in three bites. He probably shouldn't since he no longer had the excuse of daily manual labor to work off his extra snacks, but the exercise he'd engaged in with Devon and Neil late the night before last had to have counted for something. He deserved at least a half dozen for all those crunches he'd done and would happily do again sometime. He felt like he was starting to find his footing again. It was almost within reach, he could sense it.

Ms. Brown sighed. "Nothing comes to mind right away, but that is an impressive list and I'm certain good things are waiting for you just around the corner."

"You know, I'm starting to believe that too." James licked his lips. "I just need to find the right opportunity and everything will click into place."

"That's right. It will." Ms. Brown nodded sagely.

"Well, thanks again for helping out yesterday. And for hooking Mark up with the crew. It sounds like that will be exactly what he needs. Your shot is coming, kid. I can feel it." Tom matched James cookie for cookie. Now that he was retired, he and Ms. Brown informally operated a quasi-therapy kitchen right here at Hot Rods in between spending time with the family they'd made together. They sure were easy to talk to, and this obviously gave them the fulfillment James was so desperately searching for.

He could learn a lot from them and felt better having talked through his ideas.

"What are your plans for the rest of the day?" James waved his last, he swore it, half-eaten chocolate cookie at Tom.

"Well, I promised Jordan I'd take some documents up

to him at the lake house." He sighed, pretty unlike him. "I ordinarily wouldn't mind the drive, especially at this time of year when the leaves are so pretty, but Willie has a doctor's appointment and I hate to miss it."

He clasped her hand. "I'll be fine by myself, Tommy."

"I know, but—" He cut a glance to her that James couldn't quite read.

His gut clenched. Tom had lost one wife, Eli's mother, when he was young, and had only discovered another epic love with Nola and Amber's mom recently. So when she'd had a serious medical scare, it had rocked their world. Of course he wouldn't want her to go to the doctor alone. They had been traumatized and knew all too well that every moment together was precious.

James had let Tom down at the shelter, but he could handle this.

"Hey, I've got nothing to do. Besides, I'd like to check out the camera feeds and his set up for monitoring them. Why don't you let me take the stuff over to his place for you?" The mansion he shared with his country-star husband and their wife was a huge mountain hideaway complete with treehouse guest rooms and an indoor swimming pool that might as well have been its own Caribbean island. Though the trio also had a tiny house on the Hot Rides complex, where they stayed most weeknights when Wren had to work, James didn't blame them for keeping Kason's mansion in the forest for when they needed some time to themselves or room to spread out. Wayyyyy out.

"Are you sure? It'll take you most of the afternoon to make the trip there and back." Tom hesitated.

"Positive. It'll make me feel useful for two days in a row. A streak I would love to extend." James dabbed chocolate from the corners of his mouth and grinned, hoping there wasn't more lodged in his teeth.

Ms. Brown's kind smile made him feel like there probably was but that she took it as a commendation of her baking. As she should. Between her, Morgan, and Devon, James's stomach was spoiled.

Tom looked to Ms. Brown, then nodded before rising and going into the living room. He took a manila envelope out of the drawer, stuck some papers in it, and sealed it before returning and passing it to James. "I wouldn't bug you if it weren't so important." Tom winced.

"No trouble at all. Really. I'm happy to help." James snatched the envelope from Tom a little too fast to pretend that he wasn't excited by the prospect of poking around Jordan's stronghold a bit, but he didn't want Tom to change his mind.

James snagged his jacket and said his goodbyes before jogging to his car. Modern and completely stock, it looked decidedly out of place among all the gleaming, custom classic hot rods in the parking lot, but really, he was used to it at this point. He liked his cute little car just fine.

He tossed the envelope onto the passenger seat and buckled up before tooting his horn once, waving out the window to the mechanics, Tom and Ms. Brown, and even Joe, who might be able to spot James toodling away from his perch on the roof of the Hot Rods construction project behind the garage.

As James drove through the windy forest roads, he sang along to the radio, bopping in time to the music. Having a worthwhile objective really did make him feel more at ease. Besides, Tom hadn't been kidding. The views on the ride were gorgeous. The million pillars of the old trees gave way from time to time to reveal expansive vistas of the forest blanketing the valleys below and a thick river cutting through it as it winded toward the giant lake it fed at the end, which Kason's house overlooked.

James settled in, remembering that life was good and he should enjoy the little things surrounding him this day and every other. The drive passed in a blink, and soon he was waved through the guard gate outside of Kason's mountain mansion.

It must be weird to be famous. James was glad he was a simple man.

He rolled to a stop in the small lot outside the gorgeous wood-and-stone structure, taking a moment—as always—to admire the craftsmanship that had gone into the place and the way it capitalized on the scenery around it with massive walls of windows.

He knocked on the front door but no one answered, probably unable to hear him in the huge house, so used the code Tom had given him on the keypad and started peeking around, looking for his friends. "Jordan? Kason? You here?"

Wren was probably tucked into a welding helmet back at Hot Rides. But where were her guys hiding?

James checked the kitchen and the main living areas where they held most of their get-togethers before wandering deeper into the house. At the head of a hallway he didn't ever remember going down before, he heard voices. Light shone from an open doorway near the end of it.

Like a bug, he was drawn to it.

One of the rumbles, gravelly and serious as fuck, definitely belonged to Jordan. But there was another nearly as deep mixed with another man's voice—this one a seductive baritone with an accent, Indian, maybe—and a woman's too. He thought it sounded like Sola.

They seemed focused and possibly disagreeing a bit.

There was no way in hell he was leaving without delivering Tom's critical paperwork, or maybe snooping around just a bit to see what things were like inside their security team. Instead of risking hearing something he shouldn't, James decided to let them know he was there. He barged right in and waved.

"Hey, guys, what's up?" James asked loudly as he entered the room. The occupants instantly froze. Two guys James had never seen before looked at Jordan to extricate them from whatever mess he'd obviously stumbled into.

James's gaze winged from one—a big guy with tattoos that stood out on his light skin, great hair, a beard that was probably excellent for nuzzling against, and who likely owned the deep voice—to another with coppery skin and the most impressive lashes James had ever seen on a person, male or female. As he cut off, mid-sentence, James regretted the loss of his sexy accent. But the woman sitting next to her co-worker, compact yet lancing a lethal glare at James looked like she'd slice his throat if the poor bastard uttered even another syllable. He'd bet his left nut that was Sola. A couple familiar guys hovered near Jordan too: Ransom and Levi, from Hot Rides.

Which was when James realized it might not have been the best idea he'd ever had to charge right into what must be the headquarters of Jordan's security firm. The one nobody asked questions about, but everyone knew was more than a simple bodyguard biz simply because he had some odd adolescent fascination with superheroes.

After all, Random and Levi had told them that they

were in the middle of something big. And yesterday, Jordan had been polite but obviously focused on something a lot more important. Like maybe life and death important.

Oopsie daisies.

He should have turned around right then. Gone back to the living room, or even his car, and clutched the obviously top-secret papers Tom had asked him to deliver to his chest until someone came to claim them.

But instead, he opened his filter-free mouth and the worst possible thing tumbled out.

"Oh my God. Is this a murder meeting?" James's eyes bugged as his hands flew to his chest. Rather than pure horror, a sliver of intense curiosity spiked into the emotions that washed over him, making his idiotic boots take a step closer and then another. He tried to be subtle but he totally peeked over Ransom's shoulder at the map spread out on the massive table.

"Uh, we prefer to call them target assessments." Levi angled his humongous shoulders to block as much of James's view as possible.

"Oh. Okay. Well, don't let me interrupt. I'll uh, just hang out over in the corner and plug my ears until you have a free second. That looks super important." James winced then tiptoed toward a stack of papers spilling from a filing cabinet. They called to his organizational demons, making his hands itch to put them in order.

He also couldn't help but notice the gouges their guns and other spy-slash-killing paraphernalia had made in the poor wooden surface of the command center table. Wishing he hadn't left his planner in the car, he made a mental note to bring some sandpaper and varnish with him next time he visited.

Jordan looked like he was about to point toward the door, but instead he snarled then shook his head, returning to the huddle over the map of what had seemed at quick glance to be the outskirts of Middletown.

Why the hell was whatever they were cooking up so interesting to James? It seemed surreal, like one of his old comic books or those true crime dramas he couldn't get enough of on TV. Except it was wasn't fake or happening to someone he'd never heard of before. It was at least a little dangerous, which seemed exciting while he was snugly tucked into a mountain fortress, surrounded by the good guys in the equation. It tripped every one of his instincts and riled him up. These people, *they* made a real difference in the world. He was instantly envious of them and wanted to know more.

James started riffling through the documents, straightening them, sorting them into the nearby folders by topic while trying not to really absorb what they said, then sticking them back into the unit in alphabetical order. Still, no one was speaking, certainly not in the heated debate they'd been having when he arrived. Without turning to face them, James urged, "Go ahead, have your *assessment*. Just ignore me. I'll be over here fixing this mess, definitely not eavesdropping on your plans. By the way... If you don't call it a murder meeting, does that keep whatever you do from being premeditated?"

He clapped his hand over his mouth then grinned as if swearing it wouldn't happen again. "You know what. I'm going. I'll be out in the living room waiting. Sorry."

Jordan blinked a few times as if unsure how to handle him.

He rose, prepared to go, and started talking faster as a

nervous reflex. "I mean, not that I'm gonna tell anyone about what you're planning, of course. I was just wondering."

For himself, mostly. How much trouble would he be getting himself or the rest of the crew into if he followed the wild hare tromping through his better sense and offered to assist Jordan's team for more than a couple minutes?

"We're running out of time, Jordan. If we need to call in JRad or any of the specialists from the Men in Blue or our other partners, we need to get on this," the big, good-hair guy interrupted James's rambling.

Jordan mashed his temples with two fingers on each side then stabbed a finger toward James. "You. Sit down. Stop rambling. File. Don't touch anything else. Anything you hear doesn't leave this room. Not even to be shared with the rest of the Powertools. I want to ask you some more questions about the vandalism on Devon's site, but you're going to have to wait a damn minute."

Like a very obedient dog, James dropped into the seat and did as he was told.

Good-hair guy waited until Jordan hunched over the maps and disorganized papers and who knew what else on the command table before winking at James over his boss's shoulder. To his surprise, Sola was grinning in his direction too.

James flashed them a thumbs up then dug in, truly wanting to help if he could, careful to stay as quiet as he could so that he didn't distract them or remind Jordan that he was still in the room. He shouldn't have worried.

Jordan centered his attention on whatever was so critical in front of them. "Aarav, you're going to be in charge of covering our agents on the entrances and exits. I think the best vantage point would be this bluff, if it's not too far for you to feel confident."

"Come on." Aarav's gorgeous golden eyes scrunched a bit at the corners. James was glad to have another chance to hear his accent. "I could make that shot in my sleep."

"Good. Then, Sola, I need you to take care of transporting any victims we can free, then managing the safe house. And don't give me any shit about wanting to be the one to destroy...ahem...targets. Because that's a job anybody can do and protecting the women we pull out of this hellhole is the top priority. I'm trusting you with that."

Oh shit. What horrors were being inflicted on these people? James was pretty sure he didn't want to know the details about that. But he hoped like hell that these real-life superheroes, who operated on an entirely different plane from the everyday life he knew and took for granted, could put an end to it.

"So we're the anybodies, yeah?" Ransom cracked his knuckles.

"Yeah." Jordan nodded to him and Levi. "It's not going to be a fair fight, just two of you and at least seven of them."

"We've got this." Levi bumped fists with Ransom. "They'll be half drunk and who knows what else. We'll be in and out before they know we're there. Give us a little bit of cover and we'll be fine."

James's filing went way slower than it should have as his mouth hung agape, in awe of how well-oiled their operation was. Aarav, who was apparently a master sniper, was quiet but intense, whereas Sola practically vibrated with pent-up energy. Each person had their assignment and the others were relying on them to do it well in order to come out of whatever clusterfuck they were about to instigate alive.

"Sola, there's one other victim I need you to be on the lookout for."

"Aside from the women?" She whistled.

"I know. There's going to be a lot for you to do in the little time that Ransom and Levi will be cleaning the floor. I told you it was a tough one. But...it's a kid. We can't leave him behind." Jordan cleared his throat as if the possibility was especially painful for him to consider. "He's the one who gave us the tips to make the bust possible. Talked to Tom down at the youth center and finally pinpointed their location for us."

"Okay, right." Sola tapped her phone, adding notes for herself. "What's his name?"

"Mark."

James stood up then, dumping the entire sheaf of papers in his lap onto the floor. "What's he look like?"

"I thought you were forgetting everything you've heard." Jordan glared at him.

His first instinct was to apologize, but the stronger one was to take action if it meant saving someone's life instead of taking it. "I am. I am. But, I worked down at the center yesterday with a kid named Mark."

"Ah, fuck." Jordan groaned. "Why does shit like this always happen?"

He took an image, from the security camera in the youth center's hallway, and flipped it toward James. A shock of mousy brown hair fell just so over eyes he had so recently looked directly into and promised to help.

A fist of dread and urgency punched James in the gut. He staggered forward and gripped the table. "Yeah. This is him. I know him."

"If the kid is familiar with James—" Sola began.

Jordan sliced his hand through the air. "Absolutely not."

"I know you hate it, but she's right." Nolan shifted his gaze toward James, his hair still perfect despite him shaking his head. "Ransom and Levi are going in the back. They're already outnumbered. If there are a lot of people we want Sola to protect, and remove, we need a distraction. It's got to be someone they won't recognize. Someone their systems won't pick up as an operative on a scan."

James had no idea what he'd gotten himself into but he was sure it was worse than the puppy poop Mike had stepped in the other night. And he was sure Devon and Neil would hate the idea even more than Jordan did.

That didn't mean they wouldn't understand, if he explained what was at stake.

Mark! He'd obviously had a lot more going on than James had realized. No wonder he wanted to run away. And James had encouraged him to go back instead of escaping. Shit, he had to make this right,

"What would a distraction entail exactly? I pulled a few mean ding-dong-dashes when I was in high school. All Neil's idea, of course. Is that the sort of thing you're talking about?"

"What? No!" Jordan pivoted on his heel and glared at James. "Were you ever in the military?"

"Nope."

"Have any combat training?"

"Uh, not exactly. But I have taken several self-defense courses. A guy my size and...uh...as not-straight as me needed them a few times back in the day." He shrugged. "I don't like fighting, but I can take care of myself in a pinch.

It only took a few black eyes for word to get around and people to leave me alone. Well, having the rest of the crew at my back once we hit trade school probably didn't hurt either."

"He'll be fine. He's smart and quick. And he can *talk*." Ransom surprised him by taking James's side. "He's not going to have to scrap with anyone. We just need him to pretend to be a delivery guy who's dropping off a pizza to the wrong house or something. A few minutes and he'll be clear. Plus, that kid knows him. He'll be more willing to go with Sola and convince the others to do so quickly if he realizes right away that they're the good guys. If he's willing to do this, let him. His diversion will be the insurance we need to pull this off without things getting messier than they already are."

Jordan groaned as if Ransom was making sense, even if he didn't like it.

James stood three inches taller at least. Yeah, he could do that. He would just channel Neil, who could bullshit anyone. No biggie, right? Right?

Jordan propped his hands on his hips. "For the record, this is a stupid fucking idea. But we need the help. We're short-staffed with the rest of our team out on another assignment. And Mark recognizing you could be what tips the scale in our favor. So I'm not going to say no if you're intent on stepping up. Be sure."

He was. But...

"I am. I've been looking for something to do that really matters. Something that I have the skills for and could make a difference in the world. What bigger impact could I make than saving someone's—*Mark's*—life? Oh crap, that reminds me." James couldn't believe he'd almost forgotten. "I have the papers Tom was supposed to bring up here today."

"Huh?" Jordan cocked his head. "I wasn't expecting Tom. In fact, he wouldn't have interrupted us this afternoon. He knew we were in a pinch and prepping for a—"

James and Jordan hummed at the same time, their stares colliding.

James handed Jordan the envelope and the other guy tore it open. He took one look at the papers inside, snorted, and then showed them to James. "It's his goddamned electric bill."

Figured. Tom always knew what was best for them. James's presence there was a reflection of Tom's vote of confidence. It made him sure he was making the right choice.

Now James just had to make Jordan and the rest of these everyday heroes see that the Hot Rods' father figure had it right. Because suddenly he was certain. *This* was what he wanted to do with his life—stop assholes who thought they could get away with evil shenanigans for one vile reason or another.

For every bully he'd ever stood up to and whoever had hurt his sister without paying the price, he was so in, whether Jordan wanted him to be involved or not. James finally felt like he'd found his reason. Something that meant more than swinging a hammer or bringing home a paycheck. While those things had been fine when he'd also been surrounded by friends, and lovers, it didn't hold the same appeal now. This though... This could be something he could put his heart into.

"When are we doing this and what do I need to know before then?"

"Your husband and wife are going to kill me." Jordan scrubbed his hands over his face.

"It's okay, boss. You've got plenty of people to protect your fine ass." James grinned at Sola, Nolan, Aarav, Ransom, and Levi before giving them a proper toodle-loo finger wave and strutting over to join them at the table.

Or at least he would have, if his phone hadn't chosen right then to buzz in his pants, making him yelp and jump higher than a startled cat. Nolan nearly died laughing, until Jordan whacked him to get his attention back on the mission planning.

14

———————

James checked the screen of his phone. When he saw it was Neil, he cursed softly. "Shit. What time is it? I didn't tell the crew I was coming out here."

"That's probably for the best," Jordan responded. "It'd be wisest for you to leave and forget everything you heard today."

"But you're not going to force me go?" He held his breath.

"You're old enough to make your own decisions. Even if they're as awful as choosing to eat gum you find stuck to the bottom of a park bench." Jordan sighed and closed his eyes for a moment as if he couldn't believe what he was about to say. "I'm not going to lie, we could use some fresh meat as bait for this assignment and someone like you to help us get our shit together at headquarters, manage surveillance installs, handle communications during ops, and maybe a few other things in the long run. If Tom thinks you're right for the team..."

"I won't let you down." James flung himself at Jordan and wrapped around him like a boa constrictor.

Just then Kason came into the room with Wren holding his hand, and barked out a laugh. "Good thing I'm not the jealous type."

"I might be." Wren hip-checked him. "And I bet Devon could kick all of our asses. Just so you know, she's going to be here any minute. Your spouses followed me up from Hot Rides after Tom let it slip where he'd sent you, and I'm guessing the rest of your crew, like usual, isn't far behind."

"Is this Grand Central Station or a covert operation?" Jordan threw his hands up or would have if James hadn't been suffocating him. He peeled James from him, then said, "We need to get back to strategizing. I'll tell you when I know exactly what your role will be. You're responsible for breaking the news—minus a lot of details, for their own safety—to your family when they arrive. Hell, now that half of Middletown is on their way, you might as well stay for dinner and...whatever."

James narrowed his eyes at Jordan. "Does that mean you're going to interrogate them about me joining your firm?"

"Without a doubt," Kason said even as Wren nodded for Jordan. "Yep."

"They're going to be fine with it. Probably. I mean, they said they support whatever I want to do going forward." But suddenly James wasn't so sure.

"I'm sure they told you that before they realized your dream job was going to involve dangerous shit that could get you all entangled in a whole lot of trouble. Not to mention killed. That's not very likely, granted, but it's not something you should take lightly, and neither should they." Jordan grimaced. Pain flashed in his eyes even years after he'd lost his partner—whom he'd shared Wren with —to a mission gone sour.

Fortunately, neither his husband nor his wife were about to let Jordan suffer those horrible memories alone.

"It's so sexy when you save the world and try to protect the rest of us from horrible things we can't even imagine." Wren took up James's place, plastering herself to Jordan while Kason nodded and did the same on his other side. On a more serious note, Wren added, "If you think I don't worry about you, especially after what happened to Johnny, you're sadly mistaken. But I know you wouldn't be the man I love so desperately if you weren't driven to take this on. I'm sure the Powertools will feel the same way once they've had time to digest everything. Plus, being afraid for your lover's life makes welcoming them home after a rough day that much more intense."

"Oh, this job comes with groupie sex too? I'm so in." James smirked while Nolan let out a belly laugh. Even Aarav smirked behind his hand, which couldn't quite conceal his amusement. Sola sighed wistfully, obviously jealous of her boss and his two soulmates even if she would be busting Jordan's balls later for sure.

And in that moment, it all clicked into place. James felt like part of a team again. That didn't mean he wasn't a Powertool anymore, but it did mean he could be more than only that. He couldn't wait to tell the crew.

By then Neil had hung up and called back, probably freaking out, so James swiped his finger over the screen of his phone to unlock it, put it on speaker, and sing-songed, "Hello, handsome. I have some good news. I heard you're on your way here already. I can't wait to tell you about it. Plus, Jordan says you should stay for an impromptu party."

"Damn it!" Neil groaned. "I didn't pack my swimsuit and you know I've been dying to try out their indoor pool."

From nearby, Wren chuckled and said, "Darling, it's a private oasis. Bathing suits are *very* optional."

"Yes!" James could picture Neil's fist pump and the bulge in his pants since they all knew *swimming* wasn't high on the list of activities he had in mind anyway.

"See you soon. I'll explain everything then, I promise." James kissed his hand loudly then blew it toward the phone to Neil and Devon, whom he could hear asking what was going on in the background since she was probably driving.

It wasn't ten minutes later before the familiar commotion of the Powertools—minus the kids, who were apparently having a sleepover with Tom, Ms. Brown, and their honorary Hot Rods and Hot Rides cousins—stormed Kason's tranquil mountain estate.

"We're over here," James called toward the main living area.

Devon jogged down the hall and into the room. She didn't slow until she'd engulfed him in a bear hug. "When you didn't answer my calls earlier, I got nervous. You always pick up or call right back."

"Oh shit." James checked his phone more carefully and saw her attempts in the log. "I must not have had service while I was driving up here. I didn't mean to scare you." Maybe she really wouldn't be keen on him joining Jordan's team, even for boring office duty.

The rest of the crew wasn't far behind her.

"So what did you have to tell us?" Mike asked as he narrowed his eyes, taking in what was obviously the hub of Jordan's operations. Wren and Kason retreated a bit, as if trying to give them some space. Jordan and the rest of his team were still huddled over the conference table ignoring them as they had bigger shit to worry about.

"Hey, do you mind if we take over the oasis for a while?" James asked Wren and Kason.

"It's all yours." Wren grinned. "Come back when you're tired out and in need of refreshments."

James figured the crew would be less likely to argue with him in the serene and private space. Plus, if things went like he hoped, they'd be ready for phase two of his announcement.

Together they nearly trotted to the center of the mansion then down the gorgeous hand-carved staircase to the lower level and out to the rear of the house where the oasis took up a large portion of the back wall. It was made of privacy glass that provided a one-way panoramic view of the valley and lake at the bottom. But when James turned inward, he could have sworn he was on a deserted tropical island complete with a beach, palm trees, and even a waterfall. He knew from previous exploratory missions, that it concealed a secret cave containing a bar and a day bed among other things.

Figuring distractions wouldn't hurt, he didn't hesitate to strip his clothes off. He might as well be as naked in the flesh as he would be when he bared his soul to the crew, who followed suit without objection. James waded into the water with the rest of his friends and lovers right behind him. It sort of reminded him of that day they'd stormed the lake last summer. It had probably been the moment that steered them here to Middletown, though they hadn't realized it at the time.

When they were waist deep, they surrounded him, making him shiver despite the cranked heat in the oasis.

"Nowhere left to go." Neil took his hand. "Come on, what's going on?"

"Jordan has a job for me, and I want to accept it."

"Seriously?" Devon's eyes doubled in size. "Doing what?"

"Ummm, for my first day they need someone to host a little meet-and-greet, and from then on I'll probably be working in the very safe and boring headquarters here wrangling the operatives and keeping everyone in line. Not so different from what I do at home, except cooler, I guess."

"Why do I get the feeling this isn't entirely as generic as you're making it sound?" Kate turned her mom stare on him.

"Because it's not. But Jordan and the team will have my back. I mean, you saw those guys. That one, Nolan, is like a walking refrigerator—"

"But with really good hair and sexy tattoos." Neil nodded.

"Exactly!" James flung his hands out, splashing water around them. "And we're all familiar with how competent and deadly a kickass lady like Sola could be. Plus, Aarav can probably shoot your balls off from a mile away. That's even before you get to Ransom, Levi, or Jordan, and we already know they're total badasses. Would you mess with them? After this one teensy favor, I swear I won't be anywhere near the active ops going forward."

"So you're going to be some kind of ninja spy?" Devon didn't seem to think it was that odd, or unappealing either. She floated toward him and licked her lips. James's hopes lifted.

"Maybe more like Alfred, with an extra helping of panache." He laughed thinking that was about as close as he was ever going to get to actually being Robin. He'd take it. "But yeah. Whether they like it or not, they need me to organize stuff and coordinate their efforts and assist where I can. I think I could be good at this. Plus really give back, you know?"

"This isn't like dressing up as an action figure for Halloween. The bad guys Jordan takes down are real and so are their bullets." Dave asked, "You sure you don't want to be part of the Hot Rods or Hot Rides instead? They basically offered you something similar, and they're a lot safer bets."

"Don't let my cuz hear you calling him safe. Eli will think he's gone soft and feel the need to do something rebellious." Joe was probably right about the garage owner, and the rest of the mechanics too.

"I won't. And yes, I'm sure. I'm not one of their gangs. Not like I'm part of you all. I think being there every day, doing essentially the same shit I used to but without you all... It was going to make it really obvious what I was missing." James didn't want to sound like he was pouting. Hopefully, they could understand the difference.

"Then why don't you just team up with Neil or Devon? Or both, if you can't decide which to go with. You could work with whoever needs more help on whatever project they're heading up," Kayla wondered. Both Neil and Devon nodded, though James didn't.

"I'm sorry, but no. I'm not trying to be second-string anything, or to steal their thunder by being some kind of co-foreman, you know? Besides that, I want to do something intentional, with a greater purpose. You said it yourself. The stakes are high here, and that's why I want in." James realized his comment fell on an awfully quiet room when the splash of the waterfall and the gentle waves lapping against their torsos rang around them. He quickly amended, "Not that you all aren't doing important work, of course you are. But I want to spend my time on job that's fulfilling, and what I used to do isn't that for me anymore, not without you all."

"You know, I'm sure Neil is happy to fill you right up," Mike teased, waving away any lingering tension. "Just kidding. I get it. You've explained yourself plenty. We're straightforward people. We make things with our own hands, or have until now. And maybe passing that off to someone else takes away the meat of the work. The part where you're actually *doing* something."

"Yes!" James knew they would get it. "At least for me. That was what was most satisfying aside from our special break times."

He swore he wasn't going to blush at that. He was a grown man, damn it. Just because he didn't get off on overseeing laborers on a construction project didn't detract from his capability or masculinity.

"Look, it's not like any of us have particularly safe jobs. But you've never tried to keep me out of the thick of things. So, if this is what you want, go for it." Devon kissed his cheek. "Do you get to wear a cape? Oh, or maybe a finely tailored tux? I'll help you bedazzle one."

"That would be awesome, but it probably goes against Jordan's low-profile edict, damn him." James perked up. "Maybe I could at least talk him into letting me design matching polos."

Morgan snorted at that. "I wouldn't bet on it."

"So, do you think you guys could help me celebrate?" Suddenly James felt like his old self—no, even better, and more adventurous. This was exactly what he'd needed to come out of his shell, just a little. "I feel really..."

What did he feel? Relieved, excited, confident.

"Alive." James smiled so wide his cheeks hurt, or maybe he hadn't used those muscles authentically in so long they were out of shape.

"Then why don't you take charge?" Neil suggested. "Where do you want us?"

Of course his husband would understand him best.

James nodded. Then he pointed to what was either a sand bar or a miniature island not too far from their meeting spot. "Get on that beach. Stay mostly in the water but make sure you're not going to drown either. I don't want to have to call in Jordan's team to rescue anyone in the middle of really good sex."

Because he was sure that's what they were about to have.

"I guess we're going to find out if rolling around in the sand really means it gets everywhere." Kayla wasn't complaining—she took off first, leading the charge to the shallows where warm, crystal-blue water lapped the gradual incline.

"Hell yes, you are." James smacked her husband's ass. "Because tonight, I feel like being on top."

"What exactly do you have in mind?" Dave asked over his shoulder as he trailed his wife.

"You guys are going to make love to your wives, and while you do, I'm going to fuck each of you before I end up with my own spouses."

15

"**O**h damn, I like it when you're cocky." Joe made it to the gently hilled mound that protruded from the water.

Neil's hand disappeared under the surface, probably to stroke his hard-on. "That's what she said, but for the record, I totally agree."

Devon came up behind James and hopped, her legs going around his waist. He carried her piggyback to the shallows, hoping she anticipated how turned on he was going to be by the time he came back to her. She whispered in his ear, "I missed you. And this...this is a whole new you I might never have known before. I'm in favor."

She kissed him right below his ear, almost making him forget his diabolical plans. Fortunately, it didn't hurt her when he twisted, dropping her into the water with a splash. She crawled up onto the sandbar, her cute ass in the air before rolling to her back and welcoming Neil into her arms.

They made out on the beach, before grinning up at

him. Neil said, "Don't worry, I'll keep her company for you."

"Thanks." James stood watching as each of the crew paired up and got down to business. Kisses, sighs, and shortly thereafter, moans, meant they were coming together as they did best. It wasn't long until Neil fed his cock into Devon's tight pussy, making her scratch lines in the sand. So often lately it had been James inside her and Neil invading him, both of them holding him securely between them when he'd felt so damn lost, that Devon hadn't had their husband's larger cock in a while.

Tonight was going to be different. For them all.

Mike settled over Kate, Joe with Morgan, Dave on Kayla, and all of them began making love. While James could have happily stood there all night observing them, he took a detour. "Be right back."

He dove into the deeper water and swam for the waterfall. He remembered Kason telling a story about how they religiously stocked the bar with *essentials* after discovering the joys of the oasis together. James probably set an Olympic record on his way to the secret cave before dashing through the veil of cascading water, grabbing a sealed bottle of lube, and making his return journey to the crew.

Good thing, too, because they were fully engaged and ready to go when he returned.

Mike was rocking between Kate's legs, fucking her gently yet with enough speed that James figured her hormones were still in overdrive. Rather than boss James around, all eight of the lovers on the beach turned to him in anticipation when he rejoined them, waiting to see what he would do next and if he had any direction for them.

It made blood roar in his veins to know that they would bend to him, the least assertive of the bunch, without hesitation. For one night, this was what he desired.

James splashed up behind Mike, tearing the shrink wrap off the bottle of gel with his teeth even as he skidded to his knees in the sand. He didn't waste any time, or spare any lube, when he coated both his cock and Mike's ass generously. The foreman hardly ever was up for being on the bottom, and James wanted to make the best of it for both of them.

Fortunately, he wasn't as girthy as Dave or some of the other guys. Mike would be able to handle him just fine. Especially while Kate was clinging to his cock, massaging it with her wet pussy.

When James aligned his cock, Mike froze, and Kate moaned.

"You like the idea of me riding him while he's fucking you?" James asked her.

"Hell yes. It's so hot." She gazed up at him, her lips parted and cheeks flushed. "Go ahead, James. Put your dick in his ass and make him shoot so hard in me that I can't help but come too."

"Well, when you put it like that..." An involuntary clench of his muscles thrust James's hips in response to her seductive stare and the equally turned-on sighs and groans of the rest of the crew, who were witnessing his performance as they waited their turn, in response to her honesty.

They ground together, keeping each other revved and waiting for James to reach them. Their sinuous motions inspired him and he began to work into Mike's tight ass.

The foreman cursed but never stopped drilling into

Kate, so James didn't hesitate either. Hell, he couldn't stop then. Not unless Mike told him to. It felt too damn good, to be there in that moment with the people he loved most, sure that he had something to contribute to the universe. That he was worthy of them.

His stride hitched. Fuck, he hadn't realized he'd even doubted it.

"You okay?" Kate asked.

"Amazing. Perfect. Like all of you." James leaned over Mike's shoulder, driving himself balls deep as he sealed his mouth over hers in a warm and luxurious kiss.

It felt so good to bury himself in Mike over and over—their whole torsos rubbing against each other—while making out with Kate, he might have gotten carried away on the tide of passion the whole crew generated with their shared loving. Except before long, Kate began to arch and Mike started to hammer into her, impaling himself on James's cock with each backstroke.

"Sorry, James, you're going to have to find someone else to bury your cock in soon," Mike grunted out in warning moments before Kate's eyes flew open. She stared straight into James and Mike's eyes as she unraveled, writhing in the sand as she climaxed.

The milking of her pussy was too much for Mike, who roared at the artificial sky and unloaded deep inside her. His ass clenched rhythmically around James, feeling a little too good. And so, as the spasms began to dwindle, James withdrew from Mike's ass and sat on his haunches in the cool pool, catching his breath.

The waves washed over him, cleaning him off, and so when he rose from the water, he held out his hand. "Mike, toss me the lube."

The foreman seemed wrecked, unable to move or

speak, so Morgan tossed it to James. "Damn, that was so hot. I can't wait until you make Joe fly like that. I'm not going to last very long watching the two of you together."

Thank God, because James hoped he hadn't bitten off more than he could fuck. The last thing he wanted to do was disappoint Devon or Neil, though from where they were grinding against each other at the end of the line, they didn't seem to mind very much.

"You ready?" he asked Joe as he prepped his cock and the other man's ass.

"Hell yes. You're on fire today, James. Give me some of that."

When Morgan chuckled, Joe growled, then nipped her neck, making her laugh turn into a moan. "Funny, is it? We'll see what you think in a minute."

That men like these—fierce, loyal, loving, brawny-as-fuck men, would let James inside them even as they pleasured their wives, pumped him up even more than knowing what he planned to do with the rest of his life. They didn't care if he was an exclusive security team member or a stay-at-home husband—they respected him this much and always had.

James had never been so hard in his life. He sank over Joe, his cock sliding into the valley of his ass as he drizzled more slickness over them both. The last thing he wanted was to hurt one of the crew when they trusted him so completely with all that they were.

In the BC—Before Crew—era, he knew neither Mike nor Joe had ever imagined themselves bent over for a man, but now it seemed second nature in the same way it felt perfect when James came together with both Neil and Devon. He looked over at his spouses and blew them a kiss as he sank into Joe, fusing them together.

When he did, Joe bottomed out in Morgan, who hissed. Her nails dug into Joe's shoulders.

"Too much?" James asked both her and Joe.

The couple shook their heads simultaneously. Joe rasped, "Again. Do it again."

And James was happy to oblige. He pumped into Joe, who seemed even more eager than Mike had to be occupied while doing the same to his wife.

"Fuck, that feels so good." Joe tremored beneath James. "I see why you like being in the middle of Devon and Neil so much."

"You like his cock in your ass, baby?" Morgan asked. She clearly did. They all knew she only talked dirty when she was incredibly turned on.

James leaned in and captured her mouth, teasing her with swipes of his tongue that matched his pumps into her husband's tight ass. Meanwhile, Joe cursed. "It's so hot when you two kiss like that. This wouldn't be the same, you know that, right? With anyone else, this wouldn't mean so much. Feel so good."

"I love you too." James smiled at the crew, even if it looked a bit like a snarl with his face set in ecstasy.

"Damn. You better hurry, James," Dave said from his place near James's shoulder. "Kayla is so fucking hot and I can feel her getting tight on me already."

"Everyone's always tight around you, big guy," Mike teased from where he and Kate were cuddled together watching over everyone else as they found as much pleasure as the two of them had already nearly overdosed on.

Dave grunted. "True, but...not like this."

James wasn't going to rush anything. Fortunately, Morgan was every bit as affected as he was by the atmosphere, the perfect storm of taboo, open-minded, and slightly frantic sex they were sharing. She arched beneath Joe, fucking him every bit as much as James was.

She nipped James's bottom lip as she let go, but he didn't mind the sting. It kept him from tumbling over the edge with them when Joe erupted, pumping his release into Morgan even as her body did its best to draw it out of him.

James slipped from Joe's ass, splashing through the water again as he tried to catch his balance before moving on to Dave and Kayla, who were waiting for him with her open arms and his ass in the air.

Mike and Kate moved closer to Joe and Morgan, weaving into a tangle of arms and legs, their flushed skin glowing as if they had stayed in the sun too long and this had been an actual tropical island.

When James got to Dave and Kayla, he was close enough for Devon and Neil to reach out, which they did. They stroked his arm, hip, and knee as he planted them in the sand and prepared to take Dave. James huffed. "I hope you meant what you said, because I can't hold on much longer. Especially not with these two right here, doing that."

Devon and Neil grinned, not the least dissuaded. Instead they caressed him more even as they kept making love with each other.

"Yes. Now, James. Now," Kayla chanted as she spread her legs wider to make room for the two men on top of her, one of whom was mountain-sized himself. Her colorful tattoos looked even more beautiful in the simulated sunshine, dancing on her skin as she moved beneath both of them. James slathered himself and Dave with lube then slid inside, groaning when Dave's ass hugged his cock, shivering at their first contact.

James cried out, his eyes closing momentarily until Kayla kissed him gently. It was just that it was usually him, taking the rest of the guys and loving every moment. He'd forgotten what it felt like, if he'd ever known before, to realize that he could give them this pleasure too.

While tomorrow he'd probably be back to the man who enjoyed bottoming for others, this one magical night, he was going to enjoy whatever had come over him and make sure that the rest of the crew did too. James looked into Kayla's kind and understanding gaze as she reached around Dave to hug him tight. He kissed her deeply, savoring the taste of her lips as he plowed into her husband, slapping Dave's ass with his pelvis over and over.

James would probably be sore the next day and he couldn't have cared less.

Kayla smiled against his parted lips, then threw her head back, tipping into an explosive orgasm she hadn't even been able to give them a warning about. Dave seemed almost relieved when he followed her lead, shouting their names as he jerked over and over between them.

Kayla went limp, and Dave melted over her, but not James. He stood and inched backward, letting the cool water douse his desire before he approached his own husband and wife. Otherwise, they would set him on fire in an instant.

"Do you have any idea how sexy you are?" Devon asked as she bit her lip, her legs wrapped around Neil, who was fucking her relentlessly, his knees and feet buried in the sand.

"Not nearly as much as you two." James meant it. He was the luckiest man alive. When Devon unhooked her ankles to make room for James behind Neil, he put his hand over them to hold them in place. "Neil, would you mind very much if I didn't fuck you tonight? I want Devon to be in the middle this time. If... if that's what you both want too."

Devon looked up to Neil then and begged to have James. "Please, Neil. Please. We'll make it up to you next time."

"No need." Neil was already rolling to his side, taking Devon with him, his cock buried deep in her pussy. "I just want to be with you two. I don't care how or where. Just this. This is all I need."

James couldn't have resisted joining them then. He coated himself in lube again, then treated Devon to the same careful preparation, sliding his slick fingers into her one at a time until she could easily hold him without a twinge of discomfort.

The rest of the crew gathered around them, supporting them through touches and softly spoken encouragement. James fit himself to Devon, then pressed inside, groaning when she welcomed him home. Neil lifted her top leg higher, easing James's way and burrowing deeper himself.

Kayla snuck in and kissed Devon, making her shudder and arch, her body slung tight between the shuttling of James and Neil. James stared across her to Neil and then dipped his head, kissing first Devon and then Neil. And when their mouths collided, they were doomed.

They kissed each other as they gave everything they had to Devon, and the circuit was complete.

The three of them peaked together, at the center of

their crew, and rivaled the faux sun for intensity. James shot so hard he was afraid he might hurt Devon as he emptied himself inside her and Neil did the same. He could feel his husband's jerking cock through the thin tissue separating them. Devon squirmed between them as if trying to get closer to them both simultaneously.

They hung onto the blaze of rapture for what seemed like an eternity before falling back to reality together.

James would have collapsed then, but Neil and the rest of the crew were there to catch him and lower him gently to the sand where he cuddled in the middle of a ring made by Devon and the guys from the crew. The women snuggled up to their opposite sides on the outside of the ring. Right then James felt like he was at the center of their little universe, sheltered and accepted.

And he knew, he was exactly where he'd always been meant to be.

He'd nearly dozed off, the rush of the waterfall and pure satisfaction flooding him with peace, when his stomach growled. It was loud and insistent enough to sound like Moby Dick might be stalking them from the depths of the oasis.

The entire crew cracked up, laughing with him and not at him.

Devon levered herself to a sitting position, kissing the tip of his nose. "I think we might be late to dinner."

"They'll forgive us, even if they are jealous as fuck." Neil laid one last kiss on James's lips, then helped both him and Devon up. "But yeah, I have a few things I want to say to your new boss."

Heaven help them all.

16

James walked between Devon and Neil, holding one of their hands in each of his as they meandered from the oasis to the main living area of the mountain mansion. Surrounded by stone and wood beams easily as thick around as he was, James felt as secure as if they were hidden in an underground bunker. Even still, the reality of what he'd signed up for began to sink in.

He was putting himself in the line of more danger than he typically found on a construction site as a member of Jordan's team. He was pretty sure Aarav's guns shot bullets, not nails. So he understood why Neil and Devon might be worried, but he had to show them what he'd seen in just that tiny glimpse he'd gotten of their world and the utter nobility and selflessness that inspired it when he'd spied on them huddled around the table earlier.

Their energy had sucked him in even before he'd discovered that Mark truly did need him more than he'd understood.

When they rounded the corner into the living room, light glowed from the kitchen and dining room beyond. That along with the friendly banter and shit talking, which accompanied the clink of plates being set out, lured him closer.

Neil rubbed his flat stomach with his free hand. "Mmm...smells like spaghetti. I'm starving."

"Worked up an appetite in the oasis, huh?" Jordan waved them into the space. Even with his team, plus Kason and Wren, there was still plenty of room for the crew around the spacious island at the center of it.

"Hell yeah, we did." James didn't bother to hide his grin. "Worked out a few things between us too."

"So they know you've lost your mind and you're trading in your hammer for a bulletproof vest?" Jordan raised a brow, but he wasn't looking at James—he was watching Devon and Neil. "I can honestly say I don't recommend having one of your partners be in this business."

"No one's ever offered specifics, so I was smart enough not to ask until now. I'll probably regret this, but... What *is* your line of work exactly?" Neil asked, leaning against the counter.

He might have seemed casual, but James could feel the tension radiating from him. He knew the rest of Jordan's team could sense it too, because they kept cutting glances at them while dishing themselves out some spaghetti and meatballs and drawing up stools at the island. The rest of the Powertools did the same, trying to play it cool.

"Well, it's not any one thing exactly." Jordan shrugged. "Most of us have worked for governments or militaries before. We've been in situations where the right thing was obvious but not always sanctioned for various political reasons or because we were constrained by protocols and regulations. Now we work for ourselves, but we help other people slice through red tape."

"So you're vigilantes?" Devon asked.

Jordan pinched the bridge of his nose.

"What? What'd I say?" she wondered, tipping her head.

"Damn you two. First him with the M word and you with the V word." Nolan pointed at James and then Devon with his fork before scooping up a giant mouthful of pasta and downing it in a couple chomps. Must have been that learned-to-eat-fast-in-the-military thing.

"M?" Neil asked.

"Murder," James shielded his mouth from Jordan and whispered in the crew's direction. Kate dropped her fork and stared at him.

"No. That's not what we do." Aarav shook his head once. Though he spoke quietly, James could picture exactly how deadly he might be if cornered.

"Sorry." James winced.

"If someone's a terrible excuse for a human being, we make sure they can't hurt anyone else." Sola acted like they were discussing the weather as she nabbed a garlic roll out of a gorgeous hand-blown glass bowl on the island.

"Okay, well, that I can get behind." Neil looked to Dave and Kayla, who were also nodding.

James sighed dramatically. "Fine. If we're not allowed to say the M-word or anything like it, I need something better to call you than my righteous assassin buddies, which is how I'm thinking of you in my head."

Jordan cringed. "You know, we do handle situations in

a lot of different ways. Sometimes we're needed for recon or for smuggling witnesses to safe locations not even government agencies know so there's no possibility of a leak. It's only a last resort that we do...you know, *that*, really. So Cox Security Services works."

Even Morgan snorted at that. Aarav studied his meal intently.

"What?" Jordan shrugged. "I took Kason's last name when we got married."

James rolled his eyes. "Get out of here. That sounds like you're bouncers at a strip club or some shit. You need something catchy. Something we can market. I'm going to call you the Shields."

"It's not bad, actually." Nolan tapped his index finger on his lush lips, then realized he had some sauce there and licked it off. James figured if they hadn't just enjoyed themselves so thoroughly in the oasis, there might have been more than one person with too-tight pants after the maneuver.

"It has a superhero ring to it." Aarav didn't seem upset about that. "Emphasizes that what we're doing might be someone's dirty work, but it's for a good purpose."

"Don't expect me to wear fucking tights. I'm over that stage of my life." Sola tossed her long brunette hair over her slender shoulder, then propped her hand on her hip, but she wasn't vetoing the label either. James couldn't wait to get to know her better and find out what was under that tough exterior of hers. She reminded him a lot of his wife.

Devon grinned, then grabbed her dinner and took it over where Sola was sitting, hopping up on the empty stool beside her. "I like her. I can see why you chose this, James."

"So it really doesn't bother you, what we do?" Aarav

asked James quietly enough that he suspected it might sometimes bother Aarav, what they were forced to do.

"Are the people you're fucking with evil bastards?" James asked point blank.

"Yup." Nolan bobbed his head, his perfect hair never falling out of place and his bright white teeth gleaming as he grinned. Damn, he was hot.

"And are you super careful to make sure that's true before you take action?" James was a little wary about that part, but he trusted Jordan.

Jordan whipped a glare in his direction. "Of course. We only take ironclad cases and we vet every piece of intel we're given before we agree to a job. We verify what our clients tell us through several independent sources including—but you didn't hear this from me—a tech wizard named JRad from a high-caliber police squad, the Men in Blue, who can access pretty much any system in the world if he feels like it."

"What if something goes wrong and you get caught or tried for your part in these assignments?" Joe didn't seem to be one-hundred percent sold yet.

"We have written immunity agreements from most of the government agencies we work for and promises of clemency from others. Of course it's not a guarantee, there's always fucking politics to worry about, but...it doesn't behoove the people we work for to break a very valuable tool." Jordan didn't try to sugarcoat things.

James considered carefully as he scanned the crew, who seemed more concerned with stuffing their faces than anything they were hearing from the Shields. They trusted him and his gut was telling him he was meant for this. So he shrugged. "Then no, it doesn't bother me at all. Let's take out the fucking trash."

Something shifted in Aarav's gaze. Like maybe he'd never considered that someone could accept what they did, or see him as a hero instead of as a villain. James immediately wanted to play matchmaker for the dude. He wondered if he was into guys, or women, or maybe both. He added it to his mental to-do list to find out. Maybe to enlist Devon's help. They loved setting people up and had a nearly perfect track record so far. With Aarav's thick, onyx lashes and a build that said he spent a lot of time keeping active if not outright lifting weights, there would be no shortage of volunteers for the experiment.

Sola glanced at him from the corner of her eye, and James noticed her gripping her fork a little tighter than necessary, as if keeping herself from giving Aarav the hug he so desperately needed. James tucked that tidbit away in his mental files for later.

"So you get our mission. But why the hell would you choose this for yourself?" Sola asked James. "I'm sure you won't be shocked to hear that while you were busy in the oasis I combed through your personal information, including your financials. The company you own with your friends is pretty damn successful, especially lately. You don't need this kind of headache in your life."

She spun around on her stool and waited for his answer even as Jordan looked on, remaining silent and letting the Shields do the cross-examining for him. He figured on a team like this, everyone had to be comfortable or it couldn't succeed.

"Well, if you didn't do a half-assed job of your research, then you know all about my sister Laurel already." James tried not to flinch as he brought it up, but...there it was.

"Are you hoping we can help you find out what

happened to her?" Nolan wondered. "'Cause we might be good, but we probably aren't thirty-year-old-missing-person-cold-case awesome. Especially if she simply chose to leave a shitty upbringing to make herself a better life."

James sputtered. "I hadn't even considered that you would be able to find her. But now that you said it, I'd be lying if I told you I didn't wonder every damn day where she went and if she's okay. If she's happy."

Damn it. Now his eyes were burning.

He slammed them closed and took a few deep breaths before opening them, staring at the Shields and saying, "What I really want is to keep anyone else from experiencing the pain I've lived through. The injustice of it all. I know firsthand how limited some official resources are. And that's in what should have been a pretty straightforward case like Laurel's. They couldn't even spare a cop to do more than show her picture around at a few local places before assuming she took off of her own free will."

"And you doubt that she did?" Jordan asked, leaning in.

"Maybe I was naive. I was just a kid. But I think she would have let me know she was okay and come back for me if she could have instead of leaving me behind without a second thought." He reached for Neil's hand, which was already on its way to his. "Then again, maybe she never made it to a safe place where that was possible."

He cleared his throat and took a few deep breaths.

"Anyway, I've also endured my fair share of bullying and violence. If someone else is suffering worse than my sad but endurable experiences, if *someone's* life depends on us taking out a bully on steroids, then I want to help." They knew he was referring to Mark even if the rest of the crew might not. He hoped someday he could fill them in on that at least. Maybe when they'd hauled him out of whatever hellhole he was trapped in and given him a safe place to finish growing up.

"Good answer." Jordan nodded, finally plucking a plate from the stack and piling it high before taking the seat between Wren and Kason. "I'm still telling you it's not in your best interests, but... Welcome to the Shields."

James beamed, looking first to Devon and then to Neil, who both smiled back, their eyes shining with adoration and...was that pride? Damn.

Jordan wiped his mouth on a black cloth napkin. "There's a ton of shit we need some help with, starting with that mess you saw before. We could also use some new storage in the basement for our equipment. Have you ever built a gun rack before? Check with the Men in Blue if you need specs for dedicated cabinetry. I have another camera install job that's been on the backburner waiting for us to have availability. Some project management skills and communications training will help with the dispatching duties too. Amber is good at that shit. Next time you're at Hot Rods, hire her to beef up the abilities you've taught yourself organically while wrangling your crew. Offer her enough money that she can't say no. We have plenty of funding."

"Oh. Um, sure. That all sounds great." James's head was spinning.

It only rotated faster when Jordan said, "And as for this first op, stay here overnight. We'll review the detailed plan with you and get you prepped in the morning when the rest of your Powertools go back to work. But until then, I want to talk to Devon and Mike."

"Us? Why?" Devon wondered.

"Because I've got a funny feeling about the trouble at your site and I want to figure out why before we're distracted with other, more serious matters the day after tomorrow."

"A couple of teenagers screwed with my supplies because there's nothing to do in this town...yet, and now both you and James are all paranoid about it." Devon groaned.

Mike was masterminding an entertainment and tourism hub downtown that would be centered around a massive tattoo shop. Kayla's resort and spa was another part of the future they envisioned for Middletown. But James had to admit, there was mostly a lot of nature and nothing for younger residents to occupy themselves with at the moment. Maybe she was right about who had messed with her stuff.

"Could be. But something's not sitting right with me about that. Not at your site instead of Mike's. And I learned a long time ago not to ignore my gut when it tells me something." Jordan frowned.

"My gut is telling me I need another plate of spaghetti." Nolan swooped in with the giant serving spoon, and even Aarav chuckled at his antics.

But James couldn't quite shake the unease that accompanied Jordan's warning.

17

"We're heading back to Middletown. Have a good day. Rescue the world and shit!" Devon called from the main living area on the other end of the top-secret hall at the ass crack of dawn the next morning.

"First rule of this job: never let someone you care about leave without telling them you love them." Jordan jerked his chin toward the front door. James didn't argue. He jogged to the crew just in time to give Devon and Neil a hug and kiss goodbye with a little extra ass-grab for the hell of it.

"Just wait until tonight," Neil promised him. "We're going to celebrate your first day on your new job properly."

"I thought we did that last night," James fanned his face remembering their romp in the oasis.

"Well, yeah, but tonight we're going to have a private party." Devon entwined her fingers with Neil's, then dragged him away from James. "I love you."

"I love you too. Both of you. Drive safe." James sighed

as he waved and watched them descend the grand stone staircase to the parking lot through the cut-glass sidelight.

He floated back to the command center and got to work while they waited for the rest of the Shields to wake up and join them for another planning session related to the upcoming mission.

James was elbow-deep in newly created, color-coded, and organized-as-fuck files when Jordan hummed then tapped a little too hard on his laptop. He glanced over at Jordan, who didn't notice he'd drawn James's attention, in time to see him muttering curses.

"What?" James rose and crossed to Jordan, propping one ass cheek on the boardroom table and leaning in for a better look.

But what he saw sent shivers down his spine. It was Devon's construction site, as seen through one of the cameras he'd set up. "What? What's wrong?"

"The whole crew was here last night, right?" Jordan confirmed.

"Yeah." James nodded.

"And they weren't expecting any in-person deliveries or new workers during that time, right?"

"Not that I know of. And Devon would have been double and triple checking if that was the case. Why?"

"What's this trying-too-hard-to-be-inconspicuous plain white work van doing parked outside the site?" Jordan pointed.

James squashed his legs together as too many cups of coffee, or maybe nervous pee, threatened to embarrass him. "Maybe they're expecting a sub-contractor this morning."

"One who got there at two thirty-three this morning?" Jordan winged a gaze to James.

"Nope. You're right. This is fucked up." James took a deep breath.

"Don't panic. You're not about to freak out, are you?" Jordan put his hand on James's thigh. James brushed it off, then stood so he could extricate his phone from the pocket of his skinny jeans.

"Hardly." James rolled his eyes at Jordan and dialed Devon's number. No answer. "She's probably driving. Let me try Neil."

Still no answer.

"Okay, they don't have service." James clutched his phone and shooed Jordan aside so he could take control of the other man's laptop. He screenshotted the van in the driveway, then fired off an email to Tom and Eli with the subject line *URGENT – EVACUATE.*

He followed that with a brief message explaining the situation and instructed them to move their families—especially the Powertools, Hot Rods, and Hot Rides kids, who were still at Tom's house—off the premises and as far away from the mysterious van as possible. As soon as he'd done that, he opened a new tab on the browser.

"What are you doing?" Jordan asked.

"Tracking Devon's phone."

"There's no cell service..."

"What kind of super spy are you?" James glanced up at Jordan. "Just because she doesn't have cell service doesn't mean she's off the GPS grid. She has an app installed so I can see where she's at. Probably because she likes me to have her dinner ready and hot when she gets home from work."

"Are you cracking jokes right now?" Jordan raised a brow.

"Do you have a better plan?" James typed in the

website he used to access the app's data and logged in. In ten seconds flat he pointed to a glowing red dot on a map that pinpointed the location of the crew.

Jordan grinned and smacked James's shoulder. He suspected he was passing some sort of test. "I think you're going to fit in just fine here."

James went into a mode he didn't know he had. Instead of allowing himself to fall victim to fear, as he had so many times when facing down a bully, he focused. He drew on the self-defense training he'd had and started looking for ways to avoid the worst-case scenario.

Fortunately Jordan was way ahead of him. He tapped the wired phone at the center of the conference table, which apparently functioned as an intercom too, then said, "Shields, get down here. Now."

In less than twenty seconds, Nolan burst through the door, still tucking his shirt into jeans that hugged his gorgeous ass. Aarav was right behind him, looking as if he'd been ready to go for hours. He wore black boots laced nearly to his knees, and if James wasn't fueled entirely by adrenaline and hyper focused, he might have drooled.

Sola joined them, braiding the last few inches of her hair.

"Nolan, take one of Kason's souped-up motorcycles. See if you can catch the crew. They've got a serious head start on you, so I'm not sure it's possible, but do your best. Tell Ransom and Levi to follow in case you need backup."

"What's the message?" Nolan didn't bother with unimportant questions.

"Suspicious van at Devon's site. Do not approach."

Nolan nodded, then bolted from the room.

James turned back to the computer. "This van is a Ford

Econoline. Looks like it's from the early 2010s. License plate is obscured by mud, but I think I can make out the first two letters ES...."

Aarav was already popping a headset on and tapping a screen on the far side of the room. "I'll call that in to JRad and see what the Men in Blue can run for us."

"Good. What else can I check, Jordan?" James had a bad feeling as he watched the van rocking slightly on the screen. Someone was in there.

Sola had taken a seat at her station and was already clicking away at something. James didn't have to wonder what for long when an instant message popped up from her on Jordan's screen. "Take a look at that, boss."

"What is it?" Jordan asked as James double-clicked the file and opened an image that looked sort of like the one he was viewing but in shades of red that got brighter near the center of the van.

"It's the infrared setting on the camera," Sola responded.

"Heat." James winced. "Does this mean what I think?"

"I'm not about to take chances. Because, yeah, this is looking a hell of a lot like we've got a bomb on site." Jordan cursed again.

The Shields went on red alert—each of them still, quiet, and standing straight. Their simultaneous focus leveled at James was enough to knock the breath from him. If he thought the Shields were fun and easygoing, he'd misjudged them. Sure, they might be regular-ish people in their downtime, but they were honed weapons at heart. He was glad to have them on his side.

"Call it in to the local police department. Tell them you're working with me," Jordan directed James. "Then use our private coms to reach out to Nolan and update him on the situation. Tell him we'll bail him out if he gets arrested for shattering the speed limit. Then verify with Tom and Eli that everyone is off site, as far away as possible. In fact, send them to Hot Rides. Make sure Dane and Walker are there. They've both done tours in war zones and survived a notorious motorcycle club before coming to Middletown. They can handle themselves."

"On it." James tackled each task as efficiently as if his friends' lives depended on him getting them done as quickly and precisely as possible, because they might.

Jordan stood, his feet planted shoulder-width apart, his arms crossed, as each person in the room and those out in the field did their part to stop whatever was unfolding and keep it from morphing into a tragedy.

Not today, motherfuckers, James thought as he confirmed with Tom that everyone had been accounted for and moved offsite to Hot Rides. With that complete, James turned to Jordan for further instruction. He was grinning at James like a lunatic in the middle of a tornado.

"You'll do, Powertool." His amusement evaporated as a police vehicle flew into the frame of the security camera and skidded to a stop.

Cops emerged, guns drawn, presumably shouting at whoever was in the van to get the fuck out. They banged on the door with no response, but Sola had reviewed the footage from overnight. Whoever had driven that van to the site was still inside it.

Then the only thing James truly wanted to hear came through their communications device. It was Nolan, breathing hard. "I've got the crew in sight. They're about a mile away from the site. I'll divert them to the safe zone at Hot Rides."

Thank God.

"You did it." Jordan shook James hard enough to rattle his teeth. "Nice work."

Everything in him that had been buzzing with energy and drive went numb, but only for an instant. Because that's when the cops smashed the van's window and flung open its door. A man all in black rushed the cops, shoving one to the ground and bolting past them into the forest. The cops made as if to give chase until the one who'd been in the front waved the rest of them inside the van.

The instant the asshole slipped the cops and made a run for it, James was on their private channel to Nolan, Ransom, and Levi. "Perp on foot, heading west from the Bare Natural 2 site along the lakefront. Get that bastard."

Sola snorted from her station.

"What? He's a perp, right? I swear I've heard that in movies and shit."

Jordan grinned, "Yeah. Good job."

Then James opened another tab in his browser—hey, you could never have too many—and typed in the URL of the police scanner he'd learned of from the nosy neighbor group. Within a minute, he had audio to go along with their camera footage and turned it up for the rest of the Shields to hear.

The sound was scratchy and distorted but he could make out one thing clear enough: *"Send the bomb squad."*

"Fuck. I knew it!" Jordan pounded his fist into his hand. "The crew has a problem."

"Had," Aarav corrected. "Nolan will make sure they get that guy and find out who he's working for. We'll take care of this."

James nodded. They watched in relative silence as the bomb squad arrived, but after a quick peek inside, they retreated.

"Not enough time to defuse. Everyone get out." The police scanner bleeped and crackled as the cops spread the word to all their staff. People scrambled into cruisers and sped away from the destination Devon and the rest of the crew had so recently been approaching. They would have likely been on site just as...

KABOOOOOOOM.

The camera shook, was obscured by debris, then went black.

"Holy shit." Sola whistled.

James was flicking his phone's lock screen away and speed dialing Devon then. This time, thankfully, she answered. "Are you okay?"

"Thanks to you, yes." She sounded a bit wobbly, and James didn't blame her.

"I might never hear right again. Damn, and I thought a jackhammer was loud," Neil bitched in the background, making James laugh.

Thank God they were okay. Perfect. Whole. And his.

All of a sudden he got very shaky and he set his phone on the table before tapping the speakerphone button. "I love you. Stay close together, go to Hot Rides, and watch each other's backs until we know what's going on."

Jordan nodded at those directions, then squeezed James's shoulder as he disconnected. "Well, I'd say that was a hell of a first day, huh?"

"Technically that was only the first couple of hours." Aarav smirked. "We've still got a mission to plan."

"Are you going to be up for that?" Jordan asked James. "If not, we'll figure out something else. I totally understand—"

"No. No, I'm good. Nothing could scare me as bad as

that just did." James clutched his heart, impressed that he didn't also need to clean out his pants.

"I'm impressed." Sola tipped her head at him.

"So am I, and that's not easy to do." Jordan looked at James with a whole new appreciation that made him sure he was going to fit right in with the Shields.

"Boss, we got him!" Nolan's triumphant shout echoed over their communications system. "Well, I should say Ransom and Levi do. They're not playing very nice with him either."

"Motive," Jordan barked.

"Says he was hired to convince the Powertools not to stay. Didn't realize he was driving enough C4 to blow his own ass into next year. Idiot. Sounds like someone isn't a fan of the expansion plans for Middletown. Likely a competitor. We'll get the details out of him. Want us to bring him back to headquarters for questioning?"

"Yes." Jordan was stony faced, making James glad he wouldn't be part of that aspect of the operation.

"You got it, boss," Nolan confirmed. "One sorry piece of shit, coming right up."

"Where are you taking me?" a scared voice shrieked in the background. "I didn't mean to hurt anyone. Was only trying to scare them away!"

"You nearly killed innocent people." Nolan's microphone clicked. He must have shaken the asshole. "People we call friends. That was a bad life decision."

"I'm sorry, I'm sorry! What do you want to know? I'll tell you everything..."

"Yes, you will," Nolan growled, then disconnected.

"Whew!" James took off his headset, then stood, shaking his hands out. It hit him all at once, what they'd just done together. What they'd prevented from happening.

Aarav put his hand out to steady James. "Take a deep breath. You're crashing off the adrenaline. You're going to be okay, just don't pass out and bang your head or something."

"Yep. Uh huh." James bent over and stuck his head between his knees. "I'm good. Fine. Everything's fine."

"It is now," Jordan reassured him, rubbing his back. "And if you can be that coolheaded when the people you love most are in danger, you're going to be extremely valuable on the rest of our missions. You did great."

"Thanks." James stood up slowly only to find Sola and Aarav beaming at him.

"You sure you're signing up for this?" Jordan double-checked. "Sometimes being good at it isn't the same as wanting to do it, as you know already."

"*This* is what I want to do." James nodded, never more sure of anything except that he loved Neil, Devon, and the rest of the crew. "I'll learn more. I'll be useful. I swear you won't regret letting me put away sick bastards like these."

"Uh, you already did a pretty fine job this time." Aarav tried to smother a grin behind his surprisingly elegant hand. "I especially think you earned some style points when you told the cops to get their asses out to the site and not to stop for any donut breaks on the way."

James hoped he wasn't blushing too furiously. Was Aarav teasing or had he actually said that? Probably had, but it was all a blur.

"All of us have found our way here by some long and twisted roads. So...who am I to deny you an opportunity?" Jordan looked around the room, then nodded. "Everyone in favor?"

Ransom and Levi's answered over the comms immediately and in unison. "Hell yes."

Jordan turned to Aarav and Sola. She shrugged. "I already made him a log-in profile and assigned him passcodes for the security system. I'll be happy not to be the new girl anymore."

James's smile widened. This could be a new place for him to belong. For him to do something meaningful, and go home every night to his crew.

It was going to be perfect even if it was officially the scariest and most thrilling thing he'd ever attempted. Much later that afternoon, he wondered, "So what time are we reconvening for the op tomorrow night? Six a.m.?"

Aarav groaned. "Hell no. We're lazy crusaders. We don't work those kinds of hours."

"Even better." James shot them a finger wave as he turned and headed for the door. "If you'll excuse me, I have some massive thank-god-you're-safe hugs to hand out before celebrating with my wife and husband, and my crew."

"We don't need to know the details." Jordan smirked.

"Speak for yourself." Sola pouted. "I don't have two smokin' spouses and a group of lover best friends to go home to. Hell, I'd settle for one special person in my life…"

James thought there were plenty of guys, or girls if she preferred, who'd jump all over an invite like that. One of them might even be sitting right beside her, judging by the look Aarav was leveling in her direction.

18

———————

A couple of weeks later, James skipped as he finished dropping off bagged lunches to the crew with Joe at the Hot Rods renovation. Now that his schedule was a bit inconsistent and in flux, dependent on whether or not the Shields had anything cooking, he often had time to do some of the fun house-husband stuff he'd come to enjoy in the mornings before helping hunt bad guys in the afternoon and occasionally, when there were active ops, overnight. The variety suited him.

After he'd exchanged sandwiches and fresh-baked chocolate chip cookies for a bunch of hugs and a quickie with Devon beneath the cover of the now-erected skeleton of the Bare Natural 2 spa, he headed for Tom and Ms. Brown's cabin to chat with the couple, as he often did. After all, Tom had been the one to set him on this path that he was certain he'd been meant for.

"Finish playing delivery boy?" Tom teased as James dropped into one of the rockers on the porch. Ms. Brown was in the one on the other side of the guy, and all three were huddled around a cast-iron fire pit that kept them toasty while surveying their empire, despite the distinct chill in the air.

"Uh huh." James couldn't help his very obvious grin. "Gave Devon a little extra special something with her lunch."

Ms. Brown sniffed in his general direction. "You kids. You have no boundaries."

Tom chuckled and took her hand in his, chafing it to warm it. "Don't act so innocent, Willie. I know for a fact you like to make some special deliveries of your own."

"Tommy!" He earned himself a swat not only in the air but on the shoulder, making James crack up.

"You know, James, you really pulled it together. You transitioned your family out here, kept them functioning and happy, then really went for what's going to make you happy, not only for their sakes but for your own. And now you're going to do some real good in the world. Hell, you've already made an enormous difference to Mark."

"How's he doing?" James would have nightmares for a while about the conditions the boy had been living in and the sheer terror that had been etched into his face until he'd spotted James during the raid on his father's drug and prostitution empire. The instant James had wrapped his arms around Mark and hauled him from the house into the Shields' waiting get-away vehicle, flinching at the sound of every single gunshot, he'd sworn off participating in the field for good.

But just that once, he was glad he'd done it.

"He's going to be okay eventually. Ms. Rodriguez said she's probably heard a thousand times already about how cool you are and how you saved his life. He can't wait to start working with Neil and learning construction shit too. You're his hero. And I'm awfully proud of you too, kid."

"We both are," Ms. Brown added.

James felt his throat knot. When had anyone he'd valued like a mother or father said such things to him? Never. When had his parents looked at him with such esteem and joy, like Tom and Ms. Brown were right then? No other time he could recall.

"Thank you," he croaked.

"Besides, I think my son and the rest of the mechanics are a little afraid of you now, which must mean they respect the hell out of you too." Tom grinned.

James chuckled. "Well, the feeling is mutual, you know. It's pretty intimidating moving here, being a part of a community of people that I hold in very high regard, who are unbiased and accepting. Because if they have a problem with me, it's not like I can blame it on their ignorance, you know?"

"No worries about that," Tom reassured him. "You all are family. Have been for some time, but this...well, it's official now. You're never getting away from us."

James wouldn't want to if he could. He sat there in harmony with Tom and Ms. Brown, watching the kids and their puppies chase each other through the trees. Nathan and Abby, joined at the hip as always, played with Klea and Landry, along with the rest of the Hot Rods and Hot Rides children.

"They're going to be a whole next generation." James couldn't wait to see the people they grew up to be. "They'll take over half of Middletown at this rate."

Tom hummed and rocked away, the flames toasting them lightly on one side. "Even though we're heading into winter, the new year and spring will come soon enough.

Things go through seasons in life, and I think we're all ready for a whole new phase."

"I don't know, I'm kind of enjoying this one." James folded his hands over his stomach.

But he should have known that even though things had come together, there was always the possibility for unrest lurking out on the horizon.

After a few deep, calming breaths filled with the pleasant hint of campfire, his phone buzzed in his pocket. The pattern was distinct and immediately had him sitting on the edge of his chair. "It's Jordan."

"Like I said. I mean, the universe doesn't always have to prove me right." Tom shook his head but kept rocking at the same deliberate pace.

"Arrogant much, Tommy?" Willie's rebuke didn't hold much sting since her eyes twinkled when she said it. He lifted her hand and kissed her knuckles.

James answered the call. "What can I do for you, boss?"

"This time it might be about what I can do for you. Why don't you conference your spouses in on this one, huh?" The look he shot James on the videochat made his stomach do flip-flops. It only took thirty seconds or so to get Devon and Neil on the line, but that was enough anticipation for James.

"What's going on?" James asked as Jordan flipped the camera, showing them the conference table in his mountain office instead of his own face. Images were scattered across the surface where Sola, Nolan, and Aarav sat across from Jordan. "Didn't I just clean up in there?"

He stopped grousing when caught sight of a familiar flash of fawn-brown hair wrapped in a baby-blue ribbon.

It was a ponytail he'd put in his sister's hair days before she'd vanished.

"Are you okay with seeing her?" Jordan asked quietly, tracing the line of James's gaze.

He nodded. It was nice to have a reminder since lately he'd started to have trouble recalling her face and feeling shitty about himself for it.

"Just got these back from JRad at Men in Blue. Nolan had him do an age-up for us. We took the photo the police had on file of your sister and mocked up what she might look like today." Jordan zoomed in on a printout.

The air *whooshed* from James's lungs, as if someone had hit him in the gut with a two by four. Tom reached out and clasped his forearm. Devon gasped and covered her mouth, and Neil hissed a curse. The background behind Devon began to bob, and he assumed she'd started jogging up the path from her site to where he sat outside Hot Rods.

"He w-what?" James cocked his head. His hand was shaking as he reached out, his finger tracing over the photo on the screen. Down the curve of the woman's cheek and along the wavy hair. She sort of looked like him, yet not.

But those eyes. He'd know those eyes anywhere.

"If you're going to risk yourself to be one of us, this is a way we can repay you." Jordan paused then said, "If you want, we'll help you find her. Or at least find out what happened to her."

"I want." James shook as he stared, Jordan's face replacing the tantalizing image of the woman his sister might have grown into. He hoped Devon or Neil had taken a screenshot so he could pore over the image later.

"It's not all good news." Jordan cleared his throat. "The

case notes in her file make us believe the cops suspected your sister planned to run away because she got herself tangled up with some people that were 'recruiting' for human traffickers. It's a notorious organization that still exists in some form today and actually was already on our to-do list to look into."

"Who? Who did they suspect got her involved in that?" James already knew the answer.

"I'm sorry, James. Your uncle was accused of working for them, though they never did find solid evidence."

"Oh God. No. What does that mean? Someone took her? Or he *sold* her?" James held his breath. Maybe it wasn't that she'd never chosen to come back for him— maybe she couldn't.

"I'm not sure yet. But whatever we find might not be so easy to forget. We can drop it if you'd rather. I don't want to give you false hope. The odds aren't in our favor. But if nothing else, we might be able to give you some closure."

Nolan circled the table to stand in view behind Jordan, and Sola took her post at his other shoulder. Aarav joined them, nodding slowly. The four of them, plus Ransom and Levi, were badass and sincere. They were good fucking people. They would go to every end of the earth to get him answers, unlike the cops, who hadn't given much thought to a girl from the wrong side of the tracks trying to escape untold horrors way back when.

If the Shields said this could be done, he believed them.

"I want so bad." A tear rolled down his James's cheek. Devon skidded to his side just in time to dash it away, replacing it with a sweet kiss on his cheekbone. She put her arms around him and held him tight.

"Good, because we've already added it to our case list.

When you come in tomorrow, you can do more than file shit or act like you're some kind of glorified maid. You're going to help us research and trace leads. Together, we'll get this done. For better or worse, we're going to track Laurel down and make sure the people who did this to her can never hurt anyone else the same way."

Unable to speak, James nodded, then disconnected. He drew Devon into his lap and clutched her to his chest. He had everything he'd ever wanted, with the exception of that knowledge and now it was all there, within his grasp. He couldn't believe how lucky he was. He had love, security...and, finally, one hell of a purpose.

Nolan ran his hand over his hair. The nervous gesture did little to wipe away the afterimage of James's profound relief, which had been emblazoned into his mind as Jordan broke the news about James's sister. So he tried levity, mixed with a heaping helping of the truth. "I sure as hell won't mind hunting down a woman that looks like her. Damn."

He whistled as he stared at the illustration JRad had sent them. Sola smacked him in the abs with the back of her hand, but it didn't do much when faced with the eight-pack he worked on daily in Jordan's private gym.

"Sorry, sorry. It's that or I start breaking things. Thinking of what she might have gone through...it's rough."

"Well, if she's anything like James, she'll be a handful but worth it if you could hold on to her. If anyone had a chance of surviving it'd be someone like him." Aarav nodded wisely.

Sola glanced over at the sniper wistfully, making Nolan wonder if there was something going on there he hadn't noticed before. It figured—everyone had someone special but him. Before he'd met Jordan and the guy's two spouses, he wasn't sure anyone would ever sign up for the kind of relationship his instincts had always insisted would be the only sort that would work for him.

And once he'd known that finding not only a wife but a husband to share her with was possible, he figured his profession would rule out any sane partners signing on for a piece of his erratic and hazardous lifestyle.

But maybe he'd been wrong. James and Jordan both had what he'd been too afraid to dream of. It could be time for him to start looking for more than his next fight.

Nolan took his copy of the drawing Jordan had passed out to each of them, carefully folded it, and put it in his breast pocket over his heart. He patted it, vowing then and there to find the woman whose eyes called to his soul. If there was any chance of helping her at all, he would bring her back to safety and civilization. For James, to make up for the wrongs that had been done to her, and to prove to himself that someday he might be worthy of a love like his friends had found.

To see if Nolan accomplishes his goals and gets the girl (plus a guy) check out Found (Powertools: The Shields, Book 1)

If you'd like to start at the very beginning with the Powertools Crew, you can download a discounted boxset of the first six books HERE.

Yes, I know it says complete series but I wrote a seventh book more recently and haven't gotten around to updating the boxset yet, sorry!

You can find the seventh Powertools book, More the Merrier, HERE.

If you missed out on the Powertools: Hot Rods series, you can buy all eight books in a discounted single-volume boxset by clicking HERE.

To read more about the Hot Rides gang, starting with Quinn, Trevon, and Devra's story, Wild Ride, click HERE.

CLAIM A $5 GIFT CERTIFICATE

Jayne is so sure you will love her books, she'd like you to try any one of your choosing for free. Claim your $5 gift certificate by signing up for her newsletter. You'll also learn about freebies, new releases, extras, appearances, and more!

www.jaynerylon.com/newsletter

WHAT WAS YOUR FAVORITE PART?

Did you enjoy this book? If so, please leave a review and tell your friends about it. Word of mouth and online reviews are immensely helpful and greatly appreciated.

JAYNE'S SHOP

Check out Jayne's online shop for autographed print books, direct download ebooks, reading-themed apparel up to size 5XL, mugs, tote bags, notebooks, Mr. Rylon's wood (you'll have to see it for yourself!) and more.
www.jaynerylon.com/shop

LISTEN UP!

The majority of Jayne's books are also available in audio format on Audible, Amazon and iTunes.

ABOUT THE AUTHOR

Jayne Rylon is a *New York Times* and *USA Today* bestselling author who has sold more than one million books. She has received numerous industry awards including the Romantic Times Reviewers' Choice Award for Best Indie Erotic Romance and the Swirl Award, which recognizes excellence in diverse romance. She is an Honor Roll member of the Romance Writers of America. Her stories used to begin as daydreams in seemingly endless business meetings, but now she is a full time author, who employs the skills she learned from her straight-laced corporate existence in the business of writing. She lives in Ohio with her husband, the infamous Mr. Rylon, and their cat, Frodo. When she can escape her purple office, she loves to travel the world, avoid speeding tickets in her beloved Sky, SCUBA dive, hunt Pokemon, and–of course–read.

Jayne Loves To Hear From Readers
www.jaynerylon.com
contact@jaynerylon.com
PO Box 10, Pickerington, OH 43147

facebook.com/jaynerylon

twitter.com/JayneRylon

instagram.com/jaynerylon

youtube.com/jaynerylonbooks

bookbub.com/profile/jayne-rylon

amazon.com/author/jaynerylon

ALSO BY JAYNE RYLON

4-EVER

A New Adult Reverse Harem Series

4-Ever Theirs

4-Ever Mine

EVER AFTER DUET

Reverse Harem Featuring Characters From The 4-Ever Series

Fourplay

Fourkeeps

EVER & ALWAYS DUET

Reverse Harem Featuring Characters from the 4-Ever and Ever After Duets

Four Money

Four Love

POWERTOOLS: THE ORIGINAL CREW

Five Guys Who Get It On With Each Other & One Girl. Enough Said?

Kate's Crew

Morgan's Surprise

Kayla's Gift

Devon's Pair

Nailed to the Wall

Hammer it Home

More the Merrier

POWERTOOLS: HOT RODS

Powertools Spin Off. Keep up with the Crew plus...

Seven Guys & One Girl. Enough Said?

King Cobra

Mustang Sally

Super Nova

Rebel on the Run

Swinger Style

Barracuda's Heart

Touch of Amber

Long Time Coming

POWERTOOLS: HOT RIDES

Powertools and Hot Rods Spin Off.

Menage and Motorcycles

Wild Ride

Slow Ride

Hard Ride

Joy Ride

Rough Ride

POWERTOOLS: RETURN OF THE ORIGINAL CREW

The original crew is back with more steamy menage stories!

Screwed

Drilled

Grind

Pound

POWERTOOLS: THE SHIELDS

A group of undercover operatives save the world in these steamy menage stories featuring your other favorite Powertools characters

Found

Book 2

Book 3

Book 4

Book 5

MEN IN BLUE

Hot Cops Save Women In Danger

Night is Darkest

Razor's Edge

Mistress's Master

Spread Your Wings

Wounded Hearts

Bound For You

DIVEMASTERS

Sexy SCUBA Instructors By Day, Doms On A Mega-Yacht By Night

Going Down

Going Deep

Going Hard

STANDALONE

Menage

Middleman

Nice & Naughty

Contemporary

Where There's Smoke

Report For Booty

COMPASS BROTHERS

Modern Western Family Drama Plus Lots Of Steamy Sex

Northern Exposure

Southern Comfort

Eastern Ambitions

Western Ties

COMPASS GIRLS

Daughters Of The Compass Brothers Drive Their Dads Crazy And Fall In Love

Winter's Thaw

Hope Springs

Summer Fling

Falling Softly

COMPASS BOYS

Sons Of The Compass Brothers Fall In Love

Heaven on Earth

Into the Fire

Still Waters

Light as Air

PLAY DOCTOR

Naughty Sexual Psychology Experiments Anyone?

Dream Machine

Healing Touch

RED LIGHT

A Hooker Who Loves Her Job

Complete Red Light Series Boxset

FREE - Through My Window - FREE

Star

Can't Buy Love

Free For All

PICK YOUR PLEASURES

Choose Your Own Adventure Romances!

Pick Your Pleasure

Pick Your Pleasure 2

RACING FOR LOVE

MMF Menages With Race-Car Driver Heroes

Complete Series Boxset

Driven

Shifting Gears

PARANORMALS

Vampires, Witches, And A Man Trapped In A Painting

Paranormal Double Pack Boxset

Picture Perfect

Reborn

PENTHOUSE PLEASURES

Naughty Manhattanite Neighbors Find Kinky Love

Taboo

Kinky

Sinner

Mentor

ROAMING WITH THE RYLONS

Non-fiction Travelogues about Jayne & Mr. Rylon's Adventures

Australia and New Zealand